Urbane Decay

Urbane Decay

Second Edition

Michael Cieslak

Urbane Decay is published by Dragon's Roost Press.

This anthology is © 2023 Dragon's Roost Press and Michael Cieslak.

A previous version of *Urbane Decay* was published by Source Point Press 18 Dec 2018

All characters in this book are fictitious. Any resemblance to any persons living, dead, or otherwise animated is strictly coincidental.

All rights reserved. This book or any portion thereof

may not be reproduced or used in any manner whatsoever

without the express written permission of the publisher

except for the use of brief quotations in a book review.

Printed in the United States of America

Print ISBN 978-1-956824-20-9

Digital ISBN 978-1-956824-21-6

Dragon's Roost Press

2470 Hunter Rd.

Brighton, MI 48114

thedragonsroost.biz

*For all of the English teachers, editors,
and authors who encouraged and inspired me.*

Contents

INTRODUCTION	ix
AN APPROPRIATE MUSE	1
SAVING MR. HOCKEY	7
MR. HANSON GOES TO THE LAB	27
ON THE ISLAND	41
BRAINS	65
GRANDPA	67
THE CORPSE	69
BEAUTY REDEFINED	71
GREETINGS OF THE SEASON	73
THE STAIRWELL	77
DIGITAL MEDIA	87
RAGNAROK AROUND THE CLOCK	103
THE SANDWICH YEARS	115
THE PERFECT ANNIVERSARY PRESENT	117
DID YOU GET THAT?	119
CREAK	131
MR. PENNYWICKET'S TEA CUPS	147
HOLDING	153
ELLA	169
REMEDY	189
ADWENIA'S UNCONVENTIONAL OVEN	195
ABOUT THE AUTHOR	203
DRAGON'S ROOST PRESS	205
Acknowledgments	207

INTRODUCTION

Dear Devotees of the Dark,

You hold in your hands the first <u>and</u> second collection of my short fiction. A previous edition of *Urbane Decay* was released in 2018 by my good friends at Source Point Press. This new edition, available from my publishing company Dragon's Roost Press, contains new material not available in the earlier version.

Inside you will discover some of the usual suspects: zombies, ghosts, witches, and murderers, all viewed through my own twisted lens. Some of the stories appeared in previous anthologies while others are *exclusive* to this edition. I have attempted to present the stories in their original form, but it can be hard to turn off the internal editor. If I were writing them for the first time right now, I may have done things differently. However, I decided to present the material as a snapshot of the writer that was, no matter how that may bother the writer that is.

I'm not saying that they are bad the way they are. I'm just saying that once I start playing with them, I might never stop.

I hope you find this collection terrifying and entertaining.

INTRODUCTION

Enjoy the Decay,
 Michael Cieslak
 October 2023

AN APPROPRIATE MUSE

It was all gone.

He sat back in disbelief. This muse had lasted even less time than the previous one and that one, that had not even made it a week. This one was what? Three days? Was it only three days?

The pile of remains stared up at him with it's one good eye. Maggots crawled in the ragged cavern that was once an abdomen. The left arm, the skin flayed from finger tips to elbow, pointed up as if accusing him.

The damn thing was right. It was wrong to be so wasteful. There had to be something left there for him.

He leaned over to dip his pen into the red wetness of the open mouth. A few of the teeth were missing but the jaw was still in place. It smiled up at him.

It was mocking him. The censorious finger, the grin, the lone eye. They were all mocking him, his inability.

His failure.

Rage poured out of him in an incoherent scream. He stabbed down with the pen. It slashed a layer of flesh from the cheek of the corpse's face. The second swipe missed all together. This only added strength to his rage. He raised up from the char and fell upon the remains. His fists rose and fell accompanied by soft, wet sounds.

When it was over, when the dark spots retreated from him and his vision returned, he found himself on the floor. He was kneeling next to the pummeled detritus. His hands and arms were slick with gore. A dark red splatter made a fan shape on the wall. Clots of grey and black clung here and there. He ran his hands through his hair, bone splinters cascading to the floor.

He covered his face with his hands and sobbed.

He just didn't understand. When he had first started he could write for months. His first muse, why that one had lasted...

Of course that first muse had been special. It was true what they said. You always remember your first.

He closed his eyes and thought about her. A smile started to form as he remembered the way the sun had glimmered on her auburn hair. Try as he might, he had never been able to reproduce that shimmering with the florescent lights of the basement that his been his creative space at the time.

He had always had studios, dark solitary spaces where he could work on his experiments, his art. He was quite gifted. He could sculpt passably well and his painting skills had been enough to earn him a small gallery showing. Somewhere in the midwest there was a collector with not one but three of his paintings. These paintings contained the remains of not one, but two of his muses.

This was not, however, where he excelled. His real creative outlet, his real skill set, lay with the written word. If the critics were to believed his poetry was "dark and edgy," "brutal yet honest," and "the stuff of nightmares."

He was especially fond of that last one. In fact he liked it so much that he had used it as the title of his first collection of short stories. His agent had been a bit worried that it might be too presumptuous, but he held his ground. It had paid off. After *The Stuff of Nightmares* he had been able to add "award winning author" to his description.

The next pamphlet of poetry included a special one entitled "A Bit Too Presumptuous." This had been dedicated "To my friend, agent, and some time muse, thank you for the inspiration."

After that, he had needed a new agent.

That was when things had started to go so horribly wrong.

New Agent had told him he was meant for Bigger Things. New Agent told him he needed to "expand his repertoire." It was New Agent who had convinced him that he should try his hand at a novel.

The agent had been right. The novel had been a giant undertaking. The novel had been a huge success. Because of the novel he had gone on talk shows, been interviewed by members of the press, even spoken in front of groups at libraries and bookstores. People stood in line for his autograph. They waited for hours to hear him read. They asked him questions and smiled at his answers. He loved it when they asked about his inspiration.

"Where do you get your ideas?"

If they only knew.

The novel and its success had allowed him to move to his very own house in a new city in a new state.

This was good. The novel had required four muses. The four missing people, chosen at random, strangers to him and each other had finally attracted the attention of the local police.

The four bodies, when they were discovered, had attracted the attention of the FBI.

Since then, next to nothing.

He had told himself he was taking time off to bask in the success. He had told himself that he was making sure that the cops didn't have anything on him. No one had ever spoken to him about any of the muses so he assumed he had gotten off clean.

He told himself that he was not afraid. Even when he had disposed of his first editions, those beautiful hand-written pages, he had told himself he was just being prudent. He was semi-famous now. What would happen if someone were to stumble upon those original drafts?

Oh how he missed the supple bindings of those works. Only the skin of a truly flawless, truly inspiring muse went into their creation.

Anthropodermic Bibliopegy who knew there was even a word for the practice?

Caution or no, the urge to write grew within him. It built steadily, day by day, until he could resist it no more. He was still getting to know the new city. Despite this, it was easy to find the places where those who would not be missed lived and worked. The streets of the red light district were busy. The bus station was much more isolated.

The collection had been quick and flawless, just like old times.

He had written a short story and a few poems. None of them were very good, but they had been purchased sight unseen by various publishers who wanted to catch the tails of his rising star.

Since then there had been two more muses but little productivity. He knew that he had to get back on the horse. He knew he had to start work on the follow up novel if he was to avoid being labeled a one hit wonder.

He had tasted fame and it was sweet. He did not want to lose that, to slide off into obscurity.

The constant calls from the New Agent did not help matters.

"Just calling to check on my favorite wunderkid. How is that sequel coming?"

He had lied. It was coming along smoothly. Everything was great. No sophomore slump here.

It hadn't been coming along at all.

Then New Agent wanted to see something. "Just a little taste, the first few chapters."

New Agent needed to be stopped.

There was nothing he could do about New Agent himself. He had already had one agent turned muse. That had been risky and foolhardy. Repeating the process would have been outright stupid.

There was, however, an alternative. It was still risky, but less so.

That was how New Agent's lover had come to rest on the floor of his new creative space. It had been three weeks ago, three weeks of blessed silence as far as the phone calls went.

It had been a waste, as far as creativity went.

He had started the new novel. The beginning was terrible but he suffered through hoping he could fix it in the edit. He was five chapters in when he accepted what a soulless muddle it was.

He started over.

He started over again.

He scrapped the original idea and tried something different.

He acquired a new muse.

All in all he had written tens of thousands of words. Not one of them was worth keeping.

He did not know what to write. The muses were failing him.

He opened his eyes and stared at the mess he had made. He would have to clean that up soon. This one was worthless. There was no point in keeping it around. He should get rid of it and set about finding a new muse.

At least it would give him something to do while he pondered what to write. He had to do something. New Agent might not be hounding him, but his publisher or someone else would step in to take his place. Soon they would be hounding him, all of them wanting their book.

Their book.

Suddenly it hit him. That was the reason none of the muses had been inspiring him. He had lost sight of his vision. He was working for someone else. He needed to sit down and write *his* book.

He jumped to his feet, all fears gone, doubts banished. He looked at the note pad he had been scratching at. He tore the pages from it, thought better of it, and let the whole thing fall from his hand. He grabbed a new pad, fresh and full of promise. It carried no blemish of his previous failures.

He looked around for his pen. It was buried in the eye socket of the last muse. What remained of the eye was now a burst bubble sitting on its ruined cheek. He pulled it out, but the nib stayed in the skull. He did not want to waste any time so he proclaimed it lost for the moment. He would have to remember to remove it before he disposed of the remains, but that could wait. He needed to get started on his new novel.

He could not remember the last time he had felt this excited.

He practically ran to the kitchen. He returned with a tall glass filled with whiskey, a sharp knife, and a towel. He dropped the pen into the alcohol. He stared impatiently as the clear liquid became cloudy with gore. When he could wait no longer he pulled it free and dried it on the towel.

He fitted it with a brand new nib. He placed it next to the pad of paper. He breathed deeply, savoring the moment.

This new novel would be his story. Not just his as opposed to theirs, but his story. He was going to tell his special story, the story of how he had become a literary darling.

A story this important required an appropriate muse. The muse would have to be extraordinary.

He took the knife is in right hand, placed his left forearm on the table next to the towel, palm up. He drew the blade of the knife along his arm, opening a two inch cut. He watched the blood well in the cut. It oozed slowly, then began to run more freely.

He placed the towel under it, careful to not spill.

He winced, thrilled by the pain, when he dipped the pen deep into his arm.

He began to write.

SAVING MR. HOCKEY

DAVID FELT the familiar tension rising as the zombie shuffled closer. The narrow aisle slowed the creature's progress from its normal shamble to a mere crawl. The slow pace afforded David more than enough time to escape, yet he remained rooted to his seat. His stomach tightened as a cold sweat broke out across his forehead. It was a normal reaction, the standard response of the living when in close proximity to the once living. The reaction was made worse by the monster's nearness. Generally people became aware of the undead before they could approach this close. The constant moaning or, more often, the smell of decay would warn potential victims before a zombie was within striking distance. Olfactory and oratory warnings had failed David this time.

The beast, which was slowly closing on David, had been a young man at the time of its death. Its skin had taken on the sickly gray-green pallor that was common to the undead, yet the flesh was still surprisingly taunt. Zombies who reanimated after living long lives tended to decay faster. It had something to do with the elasticity of the skin and fat deposits. Overweight zombies did not last as long as thin ones. This zombie had patchy black hair matted close to its skull. It let out a low moan, an auditory early warning system, as it reached David.

When the zombie was almost upon him, David swung his feet to the right, pulling them out of the way of the push broom which the zombie slid across the floor. The zombie moaned again and continued forward. It swept the area in front of the young executive. It glanced at David, but did not move towards him. He looked into the zombie's eyes. A gray film covered the pupils. David could find no spark of intelligence behind the cloudy orbs.

He watched as the zombie janitor moved past him and down the row. A small pile of discarded cups and wrappers preceded the zombie's broom. Within a few hours, the entire arena would be cleaned and ready for the crowds already forming outside. This would be accomplished by a small army of the undead. From where he was seated, David could see the swarm of cleaning corpses. Each section had at least one of the undead sweeping, straightening, or picking up refuse. Zombie labor was slow, but it was cheap. This was why it had been retained for so long at the Joe Louis Arena. The stadium was old. It was difficult to justify the high ticket prices, regardless of how well the Red Wings were playing. It was important for the organization to cut costs wherever it could.

This was the focus of the meeting David had attended a few weeks ago. It was that meeting which had started him thinking about the plan which he would attempt later tonight. It was that plan which had him sitting in a nearly empty stadium, watching dozens of zombie groundskeepers shuffle, sweep, and straighten.

THE MEETING, two hours which had grown so important in David's mind that they warranted mental capital letters, had been weeks ago. It started with the announcement that Detroit's hockey team would be getting a new stadium. It ended with the announcement that served as the impetus for one of the craziest ideas David had ever had.

Most of The Meeting had droned by at a zombie's pace. Identical executives in expensive suits took turns offering their statistics, projections, and endless Power Point presentations. Discussions of concession revenue, skyboxes, and parking shared with the other sports teams' new stadiums buzzed around the room. Disjointed snippets from the meeting played themselves out in his mind. Isolated phrases echoed in his ears.

"Increased security means increased revenue."

"Imagine the publicity we will get when news of the mass hiring is announced."

"The new stadium will be a safe arena, a place for the movers and shakers to be seen. If this means that a bunch of rednecks with mullets have to watch the game at a bar while guzzling Molsens, so be it."

"The real fan is the one who can afford the ticket price."

When one of the speakers discussed plans for an additional stop on 'The Downtown Monorail' to accommodate the expected crowds, David stopped listening. No one from Detroit would refer to the People Mover as a monorail. Most would not bother to refer to it at all.

The drawn curtains and the lack of clocks made it impossible to determine how much time passed, but the meeting finally began to wind down. The lights rose, causing David to squint. There was a smattering of applause. A few questions were asked and fielded easily. Feeling that he should contribute somehow to the meeting, David raised his hand. After a nod from the speaker, he asked his question.

"What is the expected size of the undead labor force for the new stadium?"

Silence coalesced in the room like thickening fog. Alarmed looks flew around the mahogany table. The man in charge of the presentation glanced at his colleagues for help. His gaze came to rest on the person at the head of the table. David had no idea who this man was, but it was obvious that he was the real power in here. He oozed authority. His suit was cut just a little better, the cloth just a little more expensive than those worn by the other out of town yes-men. Unlike the others, he wore a solid gray tie which brought out the blue-gray pinstripe in the suit. It would have matched the color of his eyes, had there been any animation in them. The tie was vibrant. His eyes were cold.

He nodded. The gesture both accepted responsibility for answering David's question and dismissed the man who had been giving the presentation. The icy eyes locked on David. The man's voice was deep, hard, and unforgiving.

"There will be no zombies at the new stadium."

David had realized then that the man speaking to him was the new head of the organization. The new Skyboxes, the sushi stands, the seat warmers, were all his idea. All of the changes which would ensure that the new stadium was only a place for the elite came directly from him.

He was the kind of person David hated.

This Suit did not become head of the organization because he loved the Red Wings. He did not even care about the game of hockey. He was simply in it for the bottom line. Numbers were what he cared about. Nothing David could say would change his position.

That did not stop him from one last appeal. Although it would probably amount to nothing, David felt that he had to try.

"I appreciate what you are doing for the organization. Increased revenue will definitely help the team. I just find that I have to ask what price are we willing to pay? What are we willing to give up to make a few more dollars? Are we willing to alienate part of our fan-base just to increase our profit margin?

"Zombies have been a part of hockey forever. I remember buying my first baseball souvenir from a non-dead vendor. It was a cheap imitation jersey. This was before we sold authentic replication jerseys. I was eight years old. My uncle had managed to get tickets. Later he slipped me a twenty and told me to buy whatever I wanted. I remember my hand shaking, my heart pounding. Part of it was the thrill of the game, being there in the stadium, watching the steam of my breath. Another part was fear. I knew in the back of my mind that nothing could happen to me. The zombies were leashed and they were wearing their jaw clamps. Still, my heart pounded. I was excited and terrified."

David paused for a moment. He was suddenly aware of the other people in the room. Directly across from him, one of his coworkers was smiling, a tear welling in his eye. He nodded to David and the tear fell, making a dark stain on the Al the Octopus tie he wore. David pressed on.

"Are we going to deny that sense of wonder, that thrilling fear from a whole generation of hockey fans? Are we going to replace a tradition with dazzle? What you are talking about doing is like getting rid of that guy that used to dance while sweeping the bases during the seventh inning stretch at the old Tiger Stadium."

There was a moment of silence. There was a brief pause where David thought he just might have gotten through to the men at the other end of the table.

"What was that man's name?"

"Excuse me?" David swallowed hard.

"The sweeper, at the old stadium. What was his name?"

Too late, David realized that he had talked himself into a corner. He racked his brain for the name, but came up empty. He shook his head.

"Exactly my point. You do not know his name, and I bet that no one else in this room does either. He was once an extension of the team. Tiger fans could not imagine a baseball game without him. Now parents bring their children to baseball games and the kids get to ride the carousel. Sure, they might miss the old dancing sweeper, but that does not stop them from buying tickets.

"There is a place for traditions: the past. The old man may have been sentimental. Perhaps he just had a soft spot for the undead. Whatever the case, Mr. Pizza is no longer in control. There will be no zombies in the new stadium."

DAVID STARED out at the ice. Up where he was seated, he could barely hear the hum and whir of the Zambonis as they swept the ice. One Zamboni entered from each end of the rink. They circled the outside, then began the careful pattern that would ensure a smooth skating surface. The drivers always ran the same routes. Repetitive manual tasks which did not require problem solving skills were perfect work for zombies.

The seats began to fill with fans. Not many at first, just the die-hards who wanted to watch the teams warm-up and perhaps catch a glimpse of the Zombonies.

Normally, zombies were not allowed to operate motor vehicles of any kind due to a few horrible accidents involving zombie gardeners on riding mowers. The NHL had received a special exemption from this law by simply going ahead and training the zombies, putting them on the ice in front of hundreds of thousands of hockey fans, and then asking for permission.

The fans ate it up. It was a public relations dream. Everyone wanted to have their picture taken with one of the zombonies, as they came to be called. There was no place where this was more true than in Detroit. As the fans flowed in, David watched the number one zombie attraction in all of hockey sweep the ice: Mr. Hockey himself.

Not the actual Mr. Hockey. Gordie Howe was still alive and making commercials. No one knew who had acquired this undead worker for the team. No one knew who first noticed the uncanny resemblance between the zombie and the hockey legend. However, the marketing executive who had seized the opportunity when it presented itself had retired at age forty-five and was living on a houseboat in the Florida Keys.

Mr. Hockey, the zombie, generated an enormous amount of revenue for the team. Tee shirts bearing his likeness were stocked in the gift shop next to rest of the merchandise. Authentic jerseys bearing the number 9 and the Mr. Hockey logo outsold many of the actual team player jerseys. He was a positive symbol, an icon of both the game and the city.

And he was going to be destroyed at the end of the week.

AFTER THE MEETING there had been an official announcement regarding the new stadium. The groundbreaking had occurred, attended by a host of local celebrities and hangers-on. Work had already begun. The new home of the Red Wings would be in place for the next season.

There had been other groundbreakings as well. A mass hiring had occurred. The entertainment group now employed a host of ticket takers, concession workers, ushers, and even maintenance workers.

They were slowly being trained, or "acclimated into the new family," in the language of the new hire brochures. Editorials praised the organization for the group hiring: "Local sports team lowers local unemployment rate."

There were no headlines regarding the elimination of the zombies which were currently occupying the positions. Internal memorandum referred to "the reduction in nonliving personnel" and "the replacement of current workers by new hires." There was nothing which overtly stated that the undead staff was to be eliminated. The suits all understood. This was going to happen, there was nothing that could be done to stop it, and smart employees would not discuss it.

The more he thought about it, the more David realized he had to do something. It simply was not right to dispose of people this way, even if they were dead. Granted, people had been disposing of the their dead for the greater portion of human history, but things changed when the dead started to walk.

He did not consider himself an activist. He had never really given much thought to the "civil rights" of the undead. If anyone had asked him directly, he would have denied even thinking about the fair treatment of zombies. It was not that he thought they should be citizens. David just thought that it was not fair to destroy something that had been a loyal worker for years. It was like shooting a greyhound after it started to lose races.

He could not save them all. He realized that early on. It would be almost impossible to save even a small percentage of the nonliving personnel currently employed at the arena. He could, however, save one. It would be difficult, dangerous even. If he was caught he could kiss his career goodbye. He would be lucky to avoid prosecution.

He knew that if he did not at least try, he would not be able to sleep at night. He had to do something, make some token effort. He decided that he would rescue one zombie from destruction. That rescue would be a symbol which would allow him to hold his head above the others he worked with who sat idly by and let the loyal employees die a second time.

What better symbol than the most recognized undead employee in the Motor City? David was going to save Mr. Hockey.

The Zambonis finished their dance and left the ice. Soon the players would take the ice to begin their warm up. Fans, many of whom had been waiting in the cold for hours to see the skate-around, streamed in through the doors. David made his way back to the skybox reserved for members of the organization.

There were already a number of people in the reserved VIP box. They were all seated at the bar with their backs to the ice, watching television or talking on their cell phones. David's nod of greeting was ignored as he walked past them. He stepped out of the suite and took one of the reserved seats directly in front.

The game started. A few of the inhabitants of the skybox took seats near David. He paid little attention to them or to the game itself. Most of the people seated around him weren't watching the game either. They were talking to each other or on their ever-present cell phones. The only exception was a young blonde girl, part of the all important 'tween' demographic that the organization was trying to attract. She wore an Yzerman jersey, despite the captain's recent retirement. She spent most of the first period on her feet, cheering and watching the game through binoculars. For a change, David was as distracted as the VIPs that he despised. He made an effort to cheer when others did, but by the first intermission, he would not have known the score if not for the Jumbo-tron.

"Please direct your attention to the ice," the announcer's voice boomed. "Here come Mr. Hockey and Ted, your Detroit Red Wing Zombonies!"

A smattering of applause arose from the fans. A door at the far end of the rink opened and the two machines lumbered onto the ice. One made a quick right turn, the other headed for the opposite end.

A shiver went down David's spine. This was what he had come to see. The people around him did not realize it, but they were witnessing the second to last trip around the ice for the zombie known as Mr. Hockey.

"They are great, aren't they?"

David turned to the girl seated next to him. She held a pair of binoculars to her eyes, a wide grin on her face. He was struck suddenly by the need to tell someone about his plan. He did not need help, but he wanted someone else to know. He needed the approval of another person. He wanted someone to tell him that what he was doing was right, was brave...

...was not the most foolish thing they had every heard of.

"Do you want to take a look?"

David nodded, biting back the response which rose in his mind *I will be seeing them close enough in a little while.* He took the binoculars and peered through them.

At first, he had a hard time focusing on what he was seeing. Then he realized that that he had failed to track the Zamboni's movements. It had turned. The flat, sparkling surface in the binoculars was the ice itself. He lowered the eyepieces for a moment, got a bead on the Zamboni, and raised them once again to his eyes.

David's head snapped back in alarm. The image which grimaced out at him was horrifying. He had focused not on "Mr. Hockey," who was smoothing the ice at the far end of the rink, but the other undead Zamboni driver. Its skin was a mottled gray. In places, the flesh had sloughed off all together revealing stringy gray musculature which appeared both desiccated but strangely wet at the same time.

It had been a long time since David had seen a zombie in this condition. Reanimated workers were given regular treatments with a formaldehyde formula which kept their bodies from breaking down. Allowing a zombie to decay was bad business practice. If the body reached the point where it was no longer mobile, the zombie would be useless.

Comprehension hit David like a blow to the back of the head. The company was not going to maintain the upkeep on its zombie employees if it was going to eliminate them. The Suits would think that would be a waste of money. Instead they would continue to use the workers but do nothing to prevent their decay. When the zombies were no longer useful, they would be replaced by living workers.

It made perfect sense from a business standpoint. It would even make it easier to destroy the undead when the time came. David winced. These actions were beyond indecent. It was simply inhumane to treat any creature this way, even if it was dead.

The young executive tried to spot "Mr. Hockey" through the binoculars, but was unable to get a clear view of it. There was no way to assess the damage which the zombie had already sustained from this distance. He returned his gaze to the other zombie. It sat upright, grayish green hands gripping the steering wheel tightly. It was missing the last two fingers on its right hand. The lack of digits did not seem to affect its ability to guide the massive vehicle over the ice.

The red jersey hid most of the torso. It appeared to be fairly solid, but who knew? It could have been slowly liquefying, held together by nothing but the ribcage and wire. The shoulders, however, appeared solid. The muscles here had not decayed. Rising up from the shoulders was a matrix of heavy wire which encased the zombie's head. It appeared as if the creature had a birdcage wired over its head. This outdated safety device ensured that no one could be bitten should the worker feel a bit peckish. These cages, which resembled some medieval torture device, had been widely replaced with other safety measures. Most zombies employed by the government wore a leather face mask known as a Hannibal which obscured the lower half of the face. The military, which used zombies in a limited capacity, mostly to clear minefields, simply removed the lower jaw, making it impossible for the creatures to bite.

The National Hockey League wanted to give the illusion of dangerousness. The leather restraints did not give this impression. Something which could be restrained by a mask could not be all that worrisome. Conversely, nothing was more frightening to the public than the gaping maw of an undead creature without a jaw. It was also revolting, especially when the zombie was working one of the food service counters. The head cage was a happy medium. It provided a degree of protection while still giving the illusion of risk.

"Mr. Hockey" would be fitted with a similar cage. That, of course, would have to go. If "Mr. Hockey" were to survive in the wild, he would have to be able to fend for himself, as far as food was concerned.

THE PLAYERS RETOOK the ice and the second period commenced. David was once again lost in his plan. In his distracted state, he did not even notice the quick succession of goals scored by the home team. It took him a moment to realize that the fans were not on their feet to salute the goals, but because they were making their way to the bathrooms and concession stands. The second intermission was starting and David had barely noticed the passing of time.

He mumbled an excuse and stood as well. He practically bolted through the skybox and into the corridor beyond. He had planned on being in place by the time the zombies finished their sweep of the ice. He was already behind schedule.

He forced himself to slow to a quick walk as he proceeded down the hallway to the gray security door. This would be the first hurdle. The floor plans he had studied for the better part of a week showed this as the most direct route to his goal. If this door was alarmed or locked he would have to find another way to the subbasement. This would mean walking past the fans milling about in lines for food, drinks, souvenirs or the restrooms. It would mean passing hundreds of potential witnesses.

David paused, his sweaty palm resting on the cool handle of the door. It turned easily. He eased it open. No alarms, no bells, no security guards yelling for him to stop. He crossed the threshold and was halfway down the first flight of stairs before the door closed behind him.

David vaulted down the four flights of stairs. He reached the bottom winded, sweating, and nervous. He closed his eyes, trying to project a map of the stadium's sub-levels onto his eyelids. If he got lost now, it was all over. He could wander for hours in the dark before finding his way back. By then the stadium would be locked, the zombies safely in their pens, and his plan would have to be abandoned.

After a few tentative steps to his right, David became more sure of himself. He navigated the maze-like corridors as swiftly as he dared given the sparse illumination thrown off by caged bulbs hanging from the ceiling. He past hissing steam pipes, unmarked doors, and bare concrete floors.

He walked for ten minutes, threading his way past half seen obstacles. As he walked, one sound differentiated itself from the others. What David first mistook for the hum of machinery took on an eerie, more natural, less mechanical tone. The pitch rose and fell, yet never left the lower end of the audible register. As he walked, the sound rose in volume. The small hairs on the back of David's arms rose and he shivered.

The corridor finally ended at a thick door made of reinforced steel. The sound was loudest here. It had ceased to be a single tone and had separated into many, similar tones: low moaning, constant and unending. He had reached the zombie pens.

The door opened easily and David's senses were blitzed. The moaning had been muffled by the door. Without the barrier, his ears were besieged by the sound of the undead. Their wails washed over him, a wave of sound. In the early days of the undead uprising, it had been this constant moaning which had caused people to abandon the safety of secure locations. It had driven them mad, then driven them right into the awaiting maw of the undead.

It was too dark to see but David knew that he was in the presence of a multitude of the undead. His sense of smell told him that there were many zombies hidden by the darkness beyond. It was the stench of the grave. The smell brought to mind scavenger beasts, beetles, and blowflies. He gagged on the noxious air.

His goal was on the other side of this room. In the plans, the pens were a rough circle. He could proceed straight through to the other side, but the thought of becoming turned around in the midst of the undead was horrible. His other option was to make his way along the outside of the room. He would pass three openings, each extending outward from the center like spokes from a wheel, before reaching the one he wanted. David steeled himself and began to inch his way along the wall.

He had reached the first opening without incident. He did not see the opening so much as feel it. The air was slightly cooler, slightly sweeter. It still held the fetid rank of the undead, but it no longer burned his nostrils. He remained in this refuge for a moment before pressing on.

Somewhere between the first and second openings, the zombies became aware of his presence. The tone of their moans shifted, became louder, more urgent. David heard chains rattling, cage doors being shaken. Something threw itself against an unseen barrier a few yards from him. David strained to see into the room, but could only make out dim shapes.

He passed the second opening without stopping. He no longer worried about his plan, he no longer cared about his job. He wanted only to get away from the moaning. He wanted only to escape from the smells of rot and decomposition. He wanted to run, but was afraid he would miss the opening and end up running in a circle, trapped within the room like a hamster on a wheel.

He trailed one hand along the wall as he moved quickly. He thought he heard movement under the moaning. A person? A human guard or zombie wrangler? One of the undead, escaped from a pen? His fingertips barely detected the shift from concrete to painted steel. If the door had not been cooler he may have gone right passed it as he feared. Fortunately, this door led to the ice rink itself and was cooled by the air on the other side. He pushed it open and blinked in the harsh light. At the extreme periphery of his vision, he could see movement. He shook his head to clear his vision, then jumped to the side.

He ducked as an arm the width of a stout branch swung at his head. It missed him by inches. The hand hit the wall with a wet thud. The zombie to which it was attached was in an advanced state of decay, too far gone to work in public.

David reached the horrible revelation that if the company was no longer working to preserve their undead employees, it was unlikely that it was feeding them. The human trying to slip out of the pen could be the first morsel of food any of these zombies had encountered in weeks.

The zombie, overbalanced by its wild swing, pushed away from the wall. It reoriented itself and started again for David. A ruin of blackish liquid seeped from the monster's empty eye sockets. Science had yet to determine exactly how the undead tracked their prey. They seemed to be able to track living flesh despite the lack of eyes to see, ears to hear, or lungs to draw in scents.

However they tracked their prey, this zombie had set its sights on David.

The door had hissed closed, a pneumatic hinge forcing it shut. David shoved again at the door. It opened easily. He leapt through as the zombie lunged forward. It hit the door with a solid thump. David tried to close the door, but was unable to do so. The zombie had managed to slip one hand into the crack between the door and the wall. David gave one desperate shove and the door slammed shut. The moan on the other side rose to a wail.

David glanced down and saw what appeared to be four fat worms on the concrete floor. His stomach rolled as he realized that the zombie had sacrificed the fingers of one hand in the fight. The digits squirmed on the ground. One began to writhe towards David's shoe. He yanked his foot back, then brought it down with a grunt. He stamped the cement, squashing the fingers to gooey paste.

He leaned against the wall panting. The idea of saving "Mr. Hockey" seemed insane, especially given what he had just done to one of his zombie brethren. David thought about abandoning the plan, but to turn back now meant recrossing the zombie pens. He sighed and made his way up the hallway.

All of the halls leading to the zombie pens were slanted downwards. This made it easier to corral the undead when their shifts were over but made the walk up to the ice more of an effort.

David was once again walking towards the crowd. The second intermission was over. A roar arose from the crowd as some significant shift in play occurred. David realized dimly that he was probably missing a good game.

The air was also getting progressively cooler. The walls were painted white. Various pieces of equipment hung from hooks on the walls. David glanced at them as he walked passed. His eye caught on one of the items he thought he might need. It was a long pole with a loop of wire on one end: a zombie come-along. He grabbed it and kept walking.

The hall got progressively wider, finally opening into a large square room. There was a bank of service elevators against one wall which led to the food service areas. Opposite these was a hall which led to a ramp. At the top of the ramp was a large roll-up door.

A third hall led up to the ice. Parked here against the wall were the Zamboni machines. A few people encircled them. One had a come-along similar to the one which David held. Instead of a loop, this one ended in a hook. The hook was fastened to a ring attached to the base of "Mr. Hockey's" sternum. He pulled and the zombie slipped off of the Zamboni and fell to the floor. The other men were occupied with unhooking the second zombie from the other Zamboni. A wheeled pallet waited for the driver.

David had not planned on encountering any living people. He paused for only a moment, then strode forward, swinging the pole over his head. He brought it down hard on one of the men working on the second zombie. It caught him on the shoulder and sent him sprawling. The other two turned, startled. The one closest to "Mr. Hockey" reacted first. He let go of his come-along and snatched something from a holster at his waist. It was a small baton, similar to those used by the police. He depressed a button and blue sparks shuddered along its length.

Electricity would not kill the undead, but it would disrupt their mobility. David had no illusions as to what it would do to him. If the charge was enough to drop a zombie, it would be more than enough to stop his heart.

The man feinted forward, brandishing the stun-baton. David stabbed with the pole, but missed his assailant's arm. The heavy end of the come-along hit the floor beyond him. The man grinned and thrust at David, missing him narrowly. David backpedaled, dragging the pole with him. The wrangler stepped forward to attack again, his eyes filled with menace. The look quickly changed to one of surprise. His foot caught on the pole and he began to fall. He twisted, trying to regain his balance. He hit the concrete hard, both arms pinned below him. David stared as the man started to convulse. He turned away when he realized that his assailant had fallen on his own weapon. Smoke began to curl upwards and the air filled with the smell of ozone and burning flesh.

David turned back to the other Zamboni. One of the men, the one he had hit, had struggled to his feet. The other was racing up the ramp towards the ice. David let him go, concentrating on the one who remained. He was a squat, powerfully built man. Coarse hair covered arms crisscrossed with scars. The man grimaced at him in what may have been a smile, then lunged.

David did not think so much as react. He brought the come-along up from the floor in an arc. "High sticking," he thought, then the heavy pole connected with the side of the man's head. There was a loud crack. The short man dropped to the ground. His head bounced on the concrete with a hollow sound. Dark red liquid poured from his head. He spasmed once, then was still.

Bile burned in David's throat. He swallowed it back. He looked around the room. Four dead bodies. Two lying on the ground, one still bolted to a Zamboni, the other standing by the door. The last two regarded him with milky gray eyes. David gulped and approached "Mr. Hockey" slowly. The zombie tilted his head, regarding him like a curious dog might as the loop slipped over his head. There was a moment where it was completely still, then "Mr. Hockey" strained against the wire of his safety cage. A black tongue extended from its ruined lips and licked the gore from the end of the pole. David dropped the come-along and ran towards the rolling door.

A large red button sat half way up the wall. David hit it and the door began to ascend. To the right of the door was a pegboard covered with keys. David grabbed a ring at random. A shuffling, scraping sound caused David to turn. "Mr. Hockey" was moving towards him, the pole plowing across the floor ahead of him. David grabbed the pole and swung it to keep the zombie as far away as possible. He got the beast in front of him. The two headed up the ramp and out the door.

Three plain white vans sat at the top of the ramp next to an idling ambulance. Although rarely used, there was always an emergency vehicle on hand during a game. Most time, it just sat there unused.

When they did transport someone, it was most often a fan who was having chest pains.

"At the bottom of the ramp!" David hollered as he neared the vehicles. Two men were leaning against the side of the ambulance. One tall, one short, each smoking. Why was is that medical staff always smoked?

"There has been an accident," David said as he continued past the two. He received matching blank stares.

"People are hurt," he said slowly. "Much blood. Help them."

Mr. Hockey let out a low moan as if in agreement.

The message got through to the short one first. His eyebrows went up and the cigarette fell from his open mouth. The tall one was a little slower to respond, but at least he had the presence of mind to snub out his cigarette against the ambulance before darting inside the vehicle. The engine turned over and the ambulance headed back down the ramp.

Things were moving faster than David had expected. He had not counted on them reacting so quickly. Of course, he had not counted on the amount of bloodshed either. He had thought that someone might get hurt, but not dead. Two people, killed in order to save one undead. David fumbled with the keys. He finally found the one that unlocked the back of the first van. He opened the door, then tried to maneuver the zombie inside. As he got around to where he could use the pole to push it in, the door swung shut. He managed to pin Mr. Hockey against the van door, but no better.

David held the zombie in place and looked around to the driver's side, nothing. On the passenger side was another door. He smiled. He pulled with all his might, pivoting as he did. Mr. Hockey stumbled along at the end of the pole. David stepped quickly towards the back of the van, switching places with the zombie. It orbited David from the end of its wooden tether. David jumped into the van, pulling the pole behind him. He scrambled to the side door. It would not budge. He pulled on the handle, no movement. He felt the pole slipping from his sweaty hand. He fumbled around in the dark, finally finding the lock. The side door swung open.

David renewed his grip on the pole and yanked. He felt the

zombie resist for a moment, then stumble to the back of the van. It reached its hands out towards the man who had just saved him. Panic and claustrophobia fought for the position of chief emotion. David resisted the urge to shove the thing away and bolt. Instead he pulled. The zombie stumbled forward again, its knees hitting the rear fender of the van. The cage on its head clanged against the roof. David pulled again, feeling something pop in his back. The cage snapped from the zombie's neck and flew back into the parking lot. Mr. Hockey fell forward into the van. It began crawling towards David. He scrambled out the side door, tossing the pole back in. He slammed the door shut, then ran around to slam the back door. He felt something crash into the door just after it shut.

People were shouting from the bottom of the ramp as David drove away, his prize safely caged in the storage area of the van.

The soon to be abandoned stadium was located on the waterfront of the Detroit river, convenient to any number of freeways. The white van slipped into the northbound traffic on I-75. It passed through the revitalized areas, past the blighted neighborhoods that no one cared to revitalize, and across Eight Mile and into suburbia. Two hours later, even the northern suburbs were gone.

David had no plan for this part of the trip. He had simply intended to drive north until he was sure the area was unpopulated, drop off Mr. Hockey, then return, leaving the van in a parking lot with the keys in the ignition. This was the Motor City, an abandoned vehicle would not last long here.

This plan had hinged on stealth. In his mind, he had seen himself safely back home in his loft before anyone even discovered that Mr. Hockey was missing. David had not planned on the level of resistance that he had encountered. Nor had he expected the resistance to die. By now the State police would be looking for the van. He had to get rid of it.

"I'm sorry, buddy," he said over his shoulder.

Mr. Hockey reacted to his voice by scratching at the heavy gauge mesh which separated the cargo area from the front seats.

"I wanted to drop you off further away, where you would not be caught. I wanted to leave you someplace nice, out in the country. I just can not take that risk now."

A blue and white sign announced an upcoming rest area. David took the ramp and was delighted to see that the lot was empty. He pulled past the lights, past where there would be security cameras, and pulled over. He left the motor running and stepped out.

"I wanted to let you free somewhere where they would not get you," he said into the van. "I wanted to save at least one of you from destruction."

He sat on the rear bumper, his head in his hands.

"Now there are two people dead. Two people I killed, at least that is how everyone is going to see it. The ambulance guys saw me. They can probably give a pretty good description to the authorities. The cops are probably waiting for me back there."

David wiped his eyes and stood. He steeled himself for what he would do next. He was going to open the back door and bolt for the open driver's door. As soon as Mr. Hockey crawled out of the van, David would drive away. He might not last a long time, this close to civilization, but at least he would last longer than he would back in the city.

As he flung open the back door, an unbidden thought exploded in David's mind.

What would the zombie live on out here? He had already seen two people die, how many others would he doom by unleashing this creature on them? At the arena it was easy to forget that these were not tamed creatures. How long would it live in the wild before resorting to its natural ways?

David slammed the back door closed again. He would have to think of something else. He could not...

...he opened the back door again and stared.

The cargo area was empty.

The sliding door was open.

David took an involuntary step backwards. He sucked in a lungful of air, his body going into 'fight' mode.

The air tasted like decay.

His breath was expelled in a ragged yell as rotted teeth closed on his neck. Somehow the creature had gotten out of the van while David was sitting there talking to it. Adaptable, able to learn simple tasks, that was why the zombies had been trained in the first place.

Blood erupted from his neck and shoulder. David tried to pull away, but the zombie held him tightly. Mr. Hockey pulled his head back and came away with a mouth full of jacket, shirt, undershirt, and shoulder. David's right arm went numb. He struggled in vain as Mr. Hockey lowered his head for another bite.

David coughed. Pink foam sprayed from his lips as his body went slack. His vision dimmed, going black on the edges. He had killed two people, and unleashed this zombie to hunt countless others. And unless David got very lucky and had his spinal cord severed by one of Mr. Hockey's hickeys, he would be joining the zombie on that hunt.

MR. HANSON GOES TO THE LAB

The steel doors closed with a hiss. Representative George Hanson swallowed hard and looked at the others. Despite the fact that the elevator was easily ten feet on a side, the five men stood close enough that their shoulders were almost brushing. They followed proper elevator etiquette. Each man stood silently, watching as the numbers descended.

One man stood slightly apart from the others. The five huddled together all wore similar clothing -- dark suits, white shirts, subdued ties. The sixth man wore tan chinos. A blue hospital scrub top covered a white tee shirt. A long lab coat completed his attire. Once white, it had faded to a dingy color closer to yellowed ivory. A Rorchardt of stains dotted the front and sides.

The elevator hummed to a stop. The number read SL12. The man in the lab coat roused himself with a shake.

"Just a moment, gentlemen," he said as the doors slid open. He thumbed a button and the doors whispered closed again. He removed a key card from the pocket of the scrub top and slid it into a slot on the control panel beneath the buttons. He then leaned forward, staring at a flat black panel.

"To access the lower levels of the facility," he said without turning, "requires two forms of identification. The first is our ID badge."

He held the plastic card up for the men to see.

"The chips are an integral part of the card, making duplication almost impossible. The lift also requires an optical scan."

He tapped the glass square with the card.

"If the eyeball does not match the identity on the card, lockdown. If the card's owner does not have correct clearance, lockdown. There are a number of other security measures in place as well."

He nodded at the men. There was no need for them to know that he had also provided the security system with his thumbprint when he had closed the door. There was no need for the man to know all of their secrets.

"What happens during lockdown?" asked Hanson. He immediately regretted having asked. The other men on the Lazarus Committee had been down to the research facility on a number of occasions. He was the most recent addition to the group. This was his first visit.

Hanson turned to the wall to hide the flush that tinged his cheeks.

"Lockdown is just that, the doors to the lift lock, including the escape door in the ceiling. Then the car is pumped full of a lethal nerve agent."

They rode the rest of the way in silence.

When the doors opened, accompanied by a quiet ping, Hanson had to restrain himself from running into the hallway. He slowly filed out with the other politicians. They stepped into a small vestibule. A large door occupied the opposing wall.

The man in the lab coat stepped around the knot of men. He went straight to a handset affixed to the right wall. He spoke in quick, hushed tones. A light above the door began to flash. There was a loud hiss. The door popped into the vestibule a few inches, then swung open.

Hanson glanced at the door. It seemed comprised of layers of steel. Bolts like one would find in a bank vault were recessed into the three-inch door. At either edge was a rubber gasket that ran all the way around the door.

MR. HANSON GOES TO THE LAB

This level of the facility was airtight. It was far enough underground to be impervious to most forms of attack. It was almost impossible to break in.

More importantly, it was almost impossible to break out.

"Gentleman, welcome to zombie central."

A THIN, stooped man was waiting for them on the other side of the door. Unlike his colleague, his lab coat was pristine and buttoned to the neck. It all but glowed under the fluorescent lighting. The knot of a red tie sat in the precise center of coat's opening.

He smiled at them. The facial gesture twisted his lips upward but never touched his eyes. He ran a hand over what was left of his white hair.

"Congressmen, how good of you to join us this afternoon. For those of you who have not met me, I am Dr. Winston Gilbert. I am the head of the research department."

His voice held the slight tint of an accent. It was not so much a definition of his place of origin as a declaration of his status. Even while smiling and inviting the men further into the facility, he exuded disdain and displeasure.

"I apologize in advance for those of you who have heard this particular 'spiel' before." He emphasized 'spiel' as if trying the word on his tongue for the first time. "I tend to be a little repetitive, but I am just so proud of all that we have done here."

He led them down the hallway to a T-junction. They turned right. Behind them, the massive door slid shut with a loud thunk followed by the crash of the bolts sliding home. Hanson glanced back and was surprised to see a tiny alcove just inside the door. Sitting there was a man in a black jumpsuit and matching black cap. In his arms he cradled a very large machine gun.

Hanson and the others had walked past him without even noticing him. The young statesman vowed to be more observant as the tour continued.

The walls changed from eye wrenching white to the pale bile green found only in government buildings and institutions for the mentally ill. Hanson hurried to catch up. Dr. Gilbert continued to speak as they walked.

"These offices belong to the scientists, who you will see in a moment, who are still working to isolate the specifics of BSV. As you all know, the recent discovery of various strains of Samedi have much of the world's scientific community in an uproar."

The elected officials nodded. Collectively, they comprised the Committee for Research and Prevention of Postmortem Animation. Although this was their official title, few people referred to them thus. Early in the uprising someone had jokingly referred to them as the Lazarus Committee and the name had stuck.

They were the legislative body that made decisions that affected US policy regarding the animate deceased. As such, they were privy to information that was kept hidden from the public. One such tidbit of information was that there were different strains of the virus believed to cause zombification.

"To date we have identified 15 different strains of the Baron Samedi Virus. Researchers overseas claim to have identified as many as 22, but much of this work is unsubstantiated."

They passed through a set of double doors into an observation room. The tiled floor was replaced by lush carpeting. There were two rows of deep cushioned theater style seats. Some of the Congressmen sank into them. Others joined Dr. Gilbert at the large Plexiglas window.

Hanson stepped to the waist high railing. It appeared to be mahogany with brass fittings. The windows were set at an angle, close at floor level, then slanting outward to provide a view of the rooms below. Gilbert flipped a switch and the observation room's lighting dimmed. Those at the window could now see into the area on the other side of the glass.

The area had two dominant features. One was a long table, easily twenty feet from tip to tip. Its metal surface was scratched and dented. Two people stood at the table. Both wore baby blue biohazard containment suits. The table before them was covered with a fine layer of viscera.

Hanson felt acid rising in the back of his throat. He turned his gaze to the only other object in the room. Occupying the far wall of the room was a row of small cages. The cages were stacked five high and extended the length of the room. Hanson attempted to count them, but finally gave up. He estimated that there were one hundred cages. Most of them were occupied.

"Pan paniscus."

Hanson jumped. The voice was very close to his left ear. He had not realized Dr. Gilbert was standing so close.

"Bonobo, or Pygmy Chimpanzee. Sometimes called Gracile Chimpanzee. Possibly our closest ancestors, genetically speaking. Close enough that many feel they, along with Pan troglodytes, the Common Chimp, belong on the human branch of the evolutionary tree."

Hanson turned to look at the doctor. He did so not because he was fascinated by the information, but to avoid staring at the tiny human-like forms in their tiny cages.

"Less than 3% difference between the bonobo and human genomes, yet neither they, nor any of their primate brethren, are susceptible to BSV."

He raised his voice to address his entire audience.

"Nor are any other mammals susceptible. Not pigs, horses, cows, nor bears. Not even domesticated animals like dogs and cats that live with people who have contracted the disease. Certainly not reptiles, amphibians, fish, none of these."

He turned and looked at each man in turn.

"None of these, not even our closest ancestor," his open hand indicated the chimps below, "ever becomes a zombie."

He paused for a moment, letting the weight of the information sink in.

"We are going to find out why."

A few of the men leaned forward in their chairs. This was apparently new information.

"We are currently working on altering the structure of the virus to see if is possible to infect other animals. At this time we have evidence of BSV being carried by a host creature who shows no signs of the corresponding illness. The virus can be transmitted in this fashion, from human to chimp to another human, yet the chimp never actually contracts the illness. There are no signs of reanimation after the death of the animal."

Hanson looked up sharply.

"Is that wise?" he asked.

"Pardon?" Gilbert seemed annoyed that by the interruption. "Is what wise?"

"You are altering the virus to make it more dangerous?"

"Dangerous how?"

"At the present time, BSV only affects humans. This is a large part of the reason that the initial outbreak was not as devastating as it could have been. We were able to isolate areas, evacuate people before they became infected. Imagine how much quicker the virus would have spread if animals were contagious as well."

A murmur rose among the others in the room. Hanson heard the words "zombie dogs," spoken in low whispers.

The specificity of the virus was one of the few rays of hope that the officials had to offer. Only humans contracted BSV. There were no swarms of reanimated rats, birds, dogs, or cows. The virus was a blood borne pathogen. It could only be spread by direct contact with someone already infected who had died and reanimated. Officials shunned the word zombie, but it had taken hold in the popular lexicon. The official name of the virus did not help.

The origin of the Baron Samedi Virus, named for the voodoo Loa of death and resurrection, was unknown. Even five years after the uprising there were still no definitive facts. No one could definitively say who had first referred to it as BSV. Since that time, each new strain of the virus discovered was named after some aspect of the vooduon pantheon.

Funny how officials had embraced this categorization system, yet tried to deny what the victims were by providing them with pseudo-scientific names: Postmortem Animates, Fully-Functioning Deceased, or derogatory names: shambler, brain-munch; anything but the word zombie.

A scowl flashed across Dr. Gilbert' face. It was only there for an instant before it was replaced by a smile. That instant was enough to tell Hanson that the good doctor was not used to being questioned about his expertise, certainly not within his facility. The legislator suspected he had just fallen far from Gilbert's good graces.

"The security measures you came through to get here pale in comparison to the safety precautions utilized in the research areas."

He nodded to the scientists in their 'space suits.'

"Our decontamination procedures are well above code for this sort of thing. There is no chance that the virus is going to make it outside of the facility."

Hanson wondered who regulated the procedures for 'this sort of thing' and exactly what other things might fall in that category.

"As mentioned earlier, by determining why our nearest genetic relations are immune to BSV, we will be able to create vaccinations which produce that immunity in humans. The key to that is breaking down the chimp's immunity and modification of the virus."

Gilbert was warming to his topic again.

"Research into the development of the virus is only one of the many areas we are currently investigating. If you gentleman will follow me."

He crossed to the other end of the room. The congressmen stood and followed. Hanson looked back in the research area one more time. His gaze went past all of the shiny equipment and expensive looking machinery to the plain wire cages. He thought about the chimps he had seen in the ape habitat at a local zoo. When they weren't scampering around, swinging from artificial tree limb to artificial tree limb they sat together, grooming and caring for each other. Even at rest, they were alert, animated, in a way these animals were not. They sat; each isolated in its own cage, and stared listlessly at nothing. Some faced the rear wall. Others watched the scientists apathetically. There was no curiosity, no spark.

These chimps may not be infected with BSV, but the life in the cages had already turned them into zombies.

THE GROUP FILED out of the room. The floor had a gentle downward slope. After a few dozen feet, they were on the level of the research labs. They passed through another armed security door and into a narrow hallway. Heavy metal doors opened off the hall on both sides. Most of the doors were tightly shut. Each door had a slide plate at eye level. Dr. Gilbert stopped in front of one of the doors, slid the plate over, and peered inside.

"It is, of course, necessary to keep a limited number of test subjects on hand. While most of the post-mortem animates are kept in the large holding facility, those who are the subjects of direct testing are kept here in isolation. They can be more closely monitored by the research team and there is no danger of cross-contamination."

He stepped to one side to allow others to view the contents of the room. The first to step up, an elderly statesman from a southern state, glanced through the tiny window, then stepped away. The next, a younger representative from somewhere out east, spent considerably longer. When he finally stepped away his face was ashen. Despite this, he wore a tiny smile.

Hanson was the last in line. By the time he made it to the door, Dr. Gilbert was already leading the group away. He looked quickly into the peephole and started to move away. Then he turned slowly and returned to the window.

The room had two occupants. Both had the gray-green pallor of the undead. One of the animates had been dead for considerably longer than the other. It was in an advanced state of decay. In places the skin had rotted away completely, revealing bone and exposing viscera. It was strapped to a cot by leather straps across its forehead, chest, waist, and at each ankle and wrist.

The second animate was fresher. In the right light it could have almost passed for one of the living. While Hanson watched, the younger zombie leaned down and bit a chunk out of the stomach of the one that was tied in place. The door was soundproof, but Hanson had no problem imagining the sound of dry flesh ripping. The zombie stood, a streamer of blackish fluid drooling from its mouth. It worked its jaws a few times then stopped. It opened its mouth. The piece of flesh it had torn from its cellmate dropped to the ground.

It looked around the room, head tilted. It shuffled a few steps towards the corner. Then it snapped its head around as if seeing the helpless zombie for the first time. It walked back and bent to take another bite.

Hanson closed the door over the viewing window and ran to catch up to the group.

"What is going on in there?" he asked as soon as he was close enough to be heard.

The group stopped as one and turned to look at him. Dr. Gilbert frowned. He arched an eyebrow, then turned and continued walking.

"He just finished explaining that," whispered one of the other congressmen. "They are working on a device which causes the shamblers to try to eat each other."

"Really?"

Up to this point, no one knew why the zombies did not attack each other. Even when they gathered at a "communal food source," new-speak for a human victim, they did little more than push each other aside.

"There are a few problems," the statesman continued in a hushed tone. "The thing sends out some kind of electrical impulse, but the range is only a few feet. Whoever is wielding the thing has to be that close. At that point it is easier to just shoot the things."

"And the other problems?"

"The things only gnaw on each other. They don't go for the brain, like they would with a human. Consequently, they don't actually kill each other. Unless of course, they get lucky and bite through the spine."

"So using the machine would not eliminate the animates, just impair them?" Hanson asked. "Still, it's better than nothing."

"There is also the frequency problem. It causes some kind of brain hemorrhage thing in the user after only a few minutes."

Hanson nodded. It sounded like promising research, but it was far from being useful.

The group had stopped again. Dr. Gilbert waited for the stragglers to catch up before speaking.

"The worst of the multiple strains of BSV, the one with which we are currently most concerned, is of course, Bokor."

The group nodded. Everyone had heard of Bokor. The government had tried to keep a lid on it, but the media had gotten word. Panic had resulted.

"Every strain of the Baron Samedi Virus results in the death of the infected. How soon the victims die depends on the strain. Grand Bois is extremely virulent, but the infected can live for weeks after contracting it. Victims contracting the Loco strain hang on for so long that they are often thought to have avoided contracting BSV. On the other end of the spectrum Bacalou and Dinclinsin are very fast acting. Those contracting these strains die within hours. In the case of Dinclinsin, the death is horribly painful.

"The one thing that all of these strains of BSV have in common, other than the ultimate resurrection of the deceased, is that they eventually result in the original death of the infected. It may be hours or weeks, but eventually, the individual is going to die of BSV."

He paused for a moment. His gaze traveled over the group, seeking each man's eyes. Few held his gaze for longer than a few seconds. Hanson refused to back down. He looked into the doctor's pale blue eyes for what seemed like an eternity.

Finally, Gilbert cleared his voice and continued.

"Except for Bokor. The Bokor strain lives in the bloodstream getting stronger and stronger, but it never kills the host. In this way, it is more like a parasite than a disease. When the victim dies, however the victim dies, the corpse reanimates like any other victim of BSV."

He paused for a moment. The statesmen all wore varying looks of horror or dismay. Gilbert, on the other hand, was rapturous.

"At this point, there is no definitive test to determine whether or not someone has contracted the Bokor virus. None of the various strains of BSV are detectable in the living. It is only upon death that the virus reveals itself. After contact with the post-mortem animated, the question becomes has the person contracted BSV? If they are still alive after the normal incubation and death period, it is still possible that they have Bokor. Will they turn after death? The only way to know is to have them die.

"Now that the worst of the outbreak is under control, we have turned to looking for ways to predict post death animation. Lacking detectable physical markers, we have been forced to look for sociopsychological clues. These include specific reactions to certain stimuli."

He pressed a button on the wall and a portion of it slid down to reveal a Plexiglas window. Gilbert rapped the window.

"One way glass, just like in the televised police dramas," he said. "We have been working on various visual cues. While not every cue is appropriate for every individual, there are certain behaviors that are recognized as indicative of a high probability of post-mortem reanimation.

"These cues are identical across gender, race, and age lines."

Hanson turned his attention to the glass. On the other side was a small, brightly lit room. He was appalled to see the sole resident of the room.

A small child, perhaps nine or ten months old, sat on the middle of a small carpet. The baby wore only a diaper. A small patch of thin blonde hair stood up from its head. There was a plastic doll in the baby's hands.

"The test subject seen here is a member of a family which was attacked outside the secure perimeter ten days ago. The other members of the family all succumbed to BSV. Up to this point, the current subject has shown no evidence of infection.

"No physical evidence, that is." The doctor smiled. Hanson felt his stomach lurch.

As they watched, the baby raised the doll to its mouth and bit down. It gnawed on the doll's head for a moment, then seemed to lose interest. A few seconds later, the baby lurched forward and chomped down on the doll's head again. A stream of spittle connected the doll and the baby's mouth.

"That, gentleman, is a cranial strike. The subject is obviously attempting to eat the brains of the doll."

He pushed another button and a red light came on. A door on the far side of the room opened. Someone dressed in the familiar black combat gear of the Reanimate Termination Squad entered. The sound of the black combat boots caused the baby to turn. It stared up at the soldier, the black flak jacket, black jumpsuit, and black helmet. The baby looked up at the gas mask that hid the intruder's face and began to cry.

The wails were thin and pitiful. The small speaker below the window did not transmit the screams of a baby who was scared. They were the cries of an exhausted child.

A black-gloved hand undid the Velcro strap on a leg holster. In one smooth movement, the soldier drew a squarish firearm, chambered a round, and pointed it at the baby's head.

"No!" Hanson yelled as he ran towards the glass. He raised his hand to pound on the window. He jumped back as blood and brain matter splattered against the glass.

The baby's cries were cut short, replaced by the deafening boom of the handgun.

The soldier looked down at was left of the baby. The small corpse twitched once. The head was almost completely gone. The tiny body ended at the neck. The small hand still clutched the doll.

The trooper nudged the body with a boot. A gloved hand sliced the air in front of the armored neck in an unnecessary gesture indicating that the baby was dead. The gun was reholstered and the soldier turned and left the room. As the sliding wall obscured the window, the door opened again to admit two of the space-suited scientists.

Hanson spun on the doctor.

"What the hell is the matter with you?"

"Whatever do you mean?" Gilbert asked, seemingly unfazed.

'What do you mean, what do I mean? That was a baby!"

"It was a baby who was most likely carrying the Bokor strain of the Baron Samedi Virus."

"Most likely? You mean you don't even know?"

"How would we know? I told you all that the only way to determine infection was after death. The best that we can do with the living is to attempt to determine potential infectees via the exact physical responses which you just witnessed."

"So no one has ever verified whether or not these people have the virus?"

"How would we verify this? Kill them and see if they turn?" Gilbert stared back at Hanson. "Because that is the only way to know for sure. Perhaps you would like us to allow them to live out their natural lives in seclusion. Is that anymore humane?"

"Why not just let them live their lives and take care of them if they turn? That is a pretty big if."

"Or we could just let them go about their merry lives, possibly infecting hundreds of thousands of people until one day, through accident or natural cause, they die. Perhaps in a hospital full of helpless patients. Perhaps in an airplane full of passengers. Perhaps in the middle of a church or a school or even a government building. Then, if," he sneered at Hanson, "pretty big or not, they are infected, then they come back. Then they start attacking. Then they kill and consume and infect even more people."

He pointed at Hanson.

"Is that what you would rather? Death and exponential infection or presumptive measures, which is better? Wouldn't you rather err on the side of caution?"

"I just don't see…" Hanson began. A blur of movement caught his eye. He turned and barely had time to register the black suited Reanimate Termination Squad personnel standing there. Then lights exploded behind his eyes. His body convulsed and he fell to the floor. He looked at his arm. Two small barbs had embedded themselves there. Wires trailed back to one of the soldiers. Hanson wondered if one of them was the one who murdered the baby. He opened his mouth to ask, but did not get a chance.

Another 50,000 volts hit him and he lost consciousness.

HANSON'S TONGUE felt too thick for his mouth. He opened his eyes and sat up. The world spun around and he closed them again. Long minutes passed before the nausea passed. Finally he was able to open his eyes and look around.

He was in a small room. A mirror occupied one wall. The walls were a flat institutional beige. He stood, ignoring the vertigo, and hollered in a raspy voice.

"I am George Hanson. I am a member of the US House of Representatives. You are unlawfully holding a member of Congress!"

Dr. Gilbert's voice sounded tinny over the speaker.

"Actually, Mr. Hanson, our mandate supersedes all other laws of the country. We operate under the same freedoms afforded the Department of Homeland Security, only without any oversight."

Hanson stared at the mirror. He only saw himself. His hair was disheveled. His jacket and tie were gone. His white shirt was rumpled,

He knew that Gilbert was on the other side of the glass.

"Now just sit back and relax, Mr. Hanson. We are going to administer some tests. We will be exposing you to a number of various visual, audio, and sensory stimuli."

"Why? Why did you lock me in here?"

"We suspect that you may be carrying the Bokor strain of the Baron Samedi Virus."

Gilbert's answer was cool and even. Hanson's voice rose in alarm.

"That is preposterous. What makes you think that I am infected?"

"Well that is what we are going to attempt to determine. However, I must tell you that many of your recent statements appear to indicate the altered brain functioning which we associate with the infected."

"What statements? What are you talking about?"

"Your willingness to put the lives of the reanimated above the living, for starters. The sympathy that you showed for the reanimates."

"Potential reanimates. You don't know if that baby was infected or not."

"Of course, questioning the motives and the official policies of Postmortem Research Facility if a potential sign of infection. As is questioning the policies and motives of its director."

ON THE ISLAND

Sept 7, 2009
    11:30 p.m.
    I should really be getting some sleep.
    It is my last evening indoors, the last night I will sleep on a bed for a week. Naturally, I am wide awake. Everything has been checked and re-checked. I can't think of anything that I forgot to pack. I will even be taking this journal and a pen along.
    All right, I will admit it, I was not very jazzed about writing down my feelings, but Dr. Ross thinks it will be a good way for me to "address the experienced emotions, rather than burying or belittling them." If nothing else, I will have something to read on the boat ride back.
    I miss Janice.
    I have been doing a pretty good job of not thinking about her lately. This could be repression or it could be me moving on. I know what Ross would call it.
    She didn't really pop into my mind until after I crossed the bridge. It is only natural to think about her. Our last real vacation was the trip up here. In fact, I expect to dwell on the divorce because of that fact,

but I am not about to let the possibility of thinking about Jan deter me from doing anything.

Especially not something I have planned on doing for the last five years.

That's enough thinking about her for now. Why dwell on the past when I have tomorrow to look forward to? The television only gets one station, and that is showing the news. Some kind of industrial accident somewhere. At least I won't be tempted to stay up and watch reruns. I need to get some sleep. I have a big day ahead of me, the start of a big week.

Tomorrow I take on The Island.

Sept 8, 2009

11:00 a.m.

I am sitting on the Isle Royale Queen IV, just a little behind schedule. My journey almost ended before it began. The harbor was enveloped in dense fog. For a while it looked as if they were going to cancel the trip out, which would have been devastating.

This late in the season, there are not many people heading out to the island. In fact, there were only five other people waiting on the dock with me, two couples and another loner. We huddled in the mist sharing stories.

The first couple is young; they are big nature buffs, back-country hikers who have been to all of the major national and state parks. Their equipment was high-end, but worn in. I felt very outclassed and out of shape standing with them.

The other loner is a nature photographer. He is going to kayak around the island. I hope he is skilled. I can't imagine fighting a storm on Lake Superior in a tiny plastic canoe. This is his fourth or fifth trip here. He said he has taken a number of good moose pictures, but has yet to see a wolf.

The other couple, an older couple, is planning on spending the night at the resort. Tomorrow they take the ferry tour around the island, then return to the mainland. They seemed very excited. I did not have the heart to tell them that the "resort" is a cinderblock building which more closely resembles the dormitory of a rural college. I know because Jan and I stayed in one of the rooms when we came. We did not camp, but did a lot of hiking. The hiking took its toll. I remember sitting in an old, uncomfortable chair with ziplock bags full of ice on my knees. That was when I vowed to come back when I turned 40. Since then I have had a couple of years to whip myself into shape. Things should go a lot more smoothly this time.

That was a good trip. Jan and I hardly fought at all. At least, that is the way I remember it. Maybe nostalgia is coloring my memories.

Sept 8, 2009
6:30 p.m.
A very productive day.

The crossing was relatively smooth. After we landed, I headed straight to the Park Office. There were no problems with my reservations. My backcountry pass was all ready to go. I filled out all of the required forms then mapped out my proposed route. It is good to know that the Rangers will know where to look if I break my leg.

After that I set out for Rock Harbor campground. I was prepared to have to hike all the way out to Three Mile Campground just to get away from everyone, but I was in luck. This early in the day, few people were there. Most were packing up and heading to the docks for the return trip to the mainland. As the day progressed, a few more people arrived, but I had the area mostly to myself.

This included a welcome lack of mosquitoes. My last trip here had been in the height of the bug season. Between the mosquitoes and the horse flies, it was a nightmare. The blood from the bites never did wash out of Jan's outfit.

Well, time to boil some water and cook my dinner. I think Pad Thai tonight. I am curious to see what freeze dried Thai food tastes like.

Sept 8, 2009
11:18 p.m.
There is a radio playing just loud enough to keep waking me up. At least, I assume it is a radio. It sounds like an audio book or something. Every once and a while I catch an outburst of talking. I think it was a gunshot that woke me originally. For a moment I thought I was back in that little East Side apartment that Jan and I had when we first started dating.

Yes, it is definitely an audio book. I swear someone just said something about a corpse rising. Ridiculous. I suppose this is what I get for not hiking further in on my first night. Honestly, don't most people come here to get away from all of the lunacy? I suppose that I could say something, but...

Silence. Lovely silence. Well, not silence, but a definite lack of human sounds. It will be nice to close my eyes and fall asleep to the sounds of the trees around me.

Sept 9, 2009
12:05 p.m.
I struck camp early to make sure that I was back at Rock Harbor in time for the ferry. I slept okay, once the noise dropped off.

I must admit, I could have packed up quieter, but I took perverse pleasure in the fact that my noise was interrupting the radio owner's sleep. Jan always said I was passive aggressive.

The boat ride to the far side of the island was uneventful, but full of beautiful views. It is a shame that there are no trails which follow the southern shore all the way back. Still, it is nice to know that the trails I have chosen are usually less populated, even in the summer. Now that the boat has gone, I suspect that I will not see anyone for most of the rest of the week.

Enough stalling. Time to eat a power bar and hit the trails.

. . .

SEPT 9, 2009
6:47 p.m.

I am glad that I chose the counter clockwise route. The trek up and over the western end of the Greenstone Ridge was tougher than I expected. It is nice to know that I will be going downhill when I head back to Windigo.

The trail was quite nice and there was a wide variety of scenery. I started out at the bay, then made that hellacious climb. Yes, I am definitely still a little out of shape. Of course, I am also toting a full pack, including food and water. Shortly after I cleared the ridge, I headed into forest. I think that I saw some bark scrapings--moose?

The weirdest part of the trek was towards the end. I was hiking below the old beach lines which, according to the guide book, were caused by glaciers. It really did seem like I was hiking below the water line, very disconcerting.

It was also a little disorienting. Feldtman Lake should have been just around every bend--I was walking near beaches, after all. It was an illusion. The lake itself was still more than an hour away. I was very grateful when I reached the campsite and could stop for a while.

The campsite itself is nice. A few fire rings, a pit toilet, and some nice level ground. As expected, I have it all to myself. I set up the tent, then walked the small spur down to the big lake. According to the book, this is Rainbow Cove.

I don't see any rainbows, but as I write this I am watching a beautiful sunset over Lake Superior. I have taken a few pictures with the little camera I brought. Now I wish I had packed the good camera.

I am going to give myself a few more minutes to watch the sky change colors, then I had better head back. You always forget how truly dark the night is when you are away from all of the light pollution of the city. I would hate to twist an ankle in the dark. That would end my trip really quick.

Random Thought: The ranger at the Windigo station said something odd. As I was preparing to head out he asked if I was glad to be on the island. I said of course, I had been looking forward to it for years, ever since the last time I left. I was all prepared to tell him about my big quest in celebration of my 40th birthday, but I never got a chance.

"No, I mean away from the outbreak," he said. He pointed at the little television on the counter. It looked like CNN or Fox News, one of those stations with the permanent crawl along the bottom of the screen.

The subtitles were saying something about the numbers of infected while the picture showed rioting in some random city.

How sad. Given the chance to be out here, surrounded by the beauty of nature, and he chose to watch television. I guess nobody really appreciates what they have right in front of them.

That sounds like a lead in to some morose thoughts about failed relationships. Time to get back to the tent.

Sept 10, 2009

1:48 p.m.

Just a brief entry to jot down the incidents of this morning.

The day started off as a nice peaceful morning with birds singing in the trees overhead. Then I looked at my watch. It was almost nine in the morning! I had slept in, in fact overslept. This is the first time that this has happened in years. Even on the weekends I tend to wake up at five, certainly no later than six or six-thirty.

Breakfast was a rushed affair, eaten while striking camp. I made for the trail as soon as possible, desperate to make up for lost time. Unfortunately this meant rushing past the scenery. This was difficult to do as much of the trail has been uphill so far.

I did stop for a moment or two at the top of a knoll with a spectacular view of Feldtman Lake. I am glad that I did. As I was rummaging around for a power bar, I glanced down at the water. There, at the edge, was a moose! I managed to take a few pictures, but the telephoto on the small camera leaves a lot to be desired. You can definitely tell what it is in the picture, but the details are lacking.

I am currently sitting at Lookout Tower. It seems like I can see the whole island from up here, or at least the western half of it. I have taken a number of pictures that I hope will make good screen savers. It would be nice to be able to remember my time here alone when back in the cubicle farm.

Now is not the time to think about that. I am going to enjoy a few more minutes of solitude while finishing my lunch, then it is back to the trail.

It is so nice to be away from everyone.

Sept 10, 2009
5:18 p.m.

I made excellent time after leaving Lookout Tower. The remainder of the hike was either downhill or relatively level. A large portion of if towards the end was an empty grass plain with nothing to trip up a lone hiker's feet.

I think that the bushes I passed right before the fields were thimbleberries. I am by no means an expert on local flora, but they looked like thimbleberries. The monks at that monastery that sells jellies and jams showed them to us. That was excellent jelly. Of course, Jan hated it. To hell with her. She can eat all of the Smucker's Grape she wants.

Speaking of eating, I should set up camp and get some food in my system. Tonight I'll go for the dehydrated lasagna. I think that I liked that last time.

Note: Buying food for this trip was a pain. While there are a lot of companies that make lightweight, dehydrated food for hikers, most seem to think that no one hikes alone. The vast majority of the meals which were in stock at my local outfitter were "Meals for 2." Since I have to tote everything I don't finish off the island with the rest of my garbage, this is a real pain. I had to special order most of my dinners on-line.

What do other people do? Do they save the remains and have it for breakfast the next day? Ugh. The cook in the bag meals are a breeze to make -- just add boiling water. I have been eating right out of the bags instead of using the collapsible bowl I brought. While they are easy to prepare, this makes them very difficult to store.

At least I don't have to worry about the smell attracting bears. None live on the island.

I wonder if wolves like lasagna.

Later: Ready to turn in. Remember to inquire about that monastery when you get back to the mainland. Were they near Eagle Harbor? Do they still have any of that thimbleberry jelly?

Sept 11, 2009

7:15 p.m.

What a very strange day. It started out great but has been clouded over by…

Well, let's ignore that for now and focus on the positive things. Today's hike was spectacular. While it is less than five miles from where I camped last night at Siskiwit Bay to where I pitched my tent today at the Island Mine campground, I took most of the day to cross between the two. Instead of shlepping quickly down the trail, I took the time to enjoy the scenery.

Unlike yesterday, I started off early enough that the undergrowth was still wet with dew. Rather than soak my pant legs, I opted to walk along the shore of Siskiwit Bay. There, in the sand, was a trail of paw prints. At first I wrote it off. I can't count the number of times I have come across the twin tracks of a dog and its owner while walking in the morning. In the months that I took to prepare for this outing I must have come across hundreds.

These, however, were a little different. For one thing, there were no human footprints next to them. However, the paw prints were close to the water line, so I assumed that the incoming tide had washed away the signs left by the dog's owner. Indeed, the water was starting to erase the prints left by the big dog.

Then it hit me. No pets are allowed on the island; something about passing disease on to the wildlife.

So if these were not the prints of a big dog, they had to have been left by a wolf!

ON THE ISLAND

I would love to say that I quietly and patiently tracked the prints to their owner, then crept closer, ever so slowly, and approached until I was within camera range.

That would be a lie.

In fact, once I realized that I was following the path of a wolf, a strange terror took hold of me. Rationally, I knew that the chances of seeing a wolf, despite the secure population which lives on the island, were slim to none. But isn't that what they said about seeing moose? I had already seen one of them. What would a wolf do if I came across it? Probably run. I knew this, but fear still gripped my heart. I headed back up to the trail proper, wet undergrowth or no. I paused only long enough to take a few shaky pictures of the paw prints.

Now I wish I had had the courage to follow the tracks, at least for a little while.

Dr. Ross said this should be a "no regrets" trip. Besides, I saw plenty of other interesting (and photograph worthy!) things on the trail.

The first thing that I passed was the remains of a stone building. According to a small sign nearby, this is where the mining company had stored their explosives. A little further up the trail was one of the mines. I did not explore too much, as the guide book noted that there are still drop-offs waiting to catch unwary travelers.

The most spectacular part of the day which ended up being photographed the most, was the subtle change in trees. Just past the mine was a stream or tributary of some river. I will have to look it up later. Up to this point I had been following a smooth path which was probably one of the old mining roads, now taken over by vegetation. The trees were mainly of the evergreen variety, probably spruce and fir. I gauge this only by the Christmas trees I have purchased in the past. There were also a number of those paper bark trees that I used to strip to make little canoes when I was a kid.

On the other side of the stream, the trees suddenly changed. The deep greens of the evergreens were replaced by a riot of bright reds, yellows, and oranges. As I wrote before, I am no expert on vegetation, but even I know a sugar maple when I see one. I think the others were some kind of oaks.

I am so glad that I delayed coming here until the fall. While the differences between the forests would have been noticeable in the summer, the abrupt and unexpected blast of color was amazing.

In the midst of all of this color was the Island Mine campground. I could spend the night here or head back to Windigo another 6 miles down the trail. While sitting in my apartment looking at maps I could not decide which to choose. Standing in the middle of the beautiful fall colors, there was no choice to make.

I almost wish now that I had continued on. Then I would not have met Stan and Cindy.

Even with my side trips, I made it to the Island Mine Campground with plenty of daylight left. I set up my tent then collected and purified some water. I was finding the dehydrated dinners difficult enough to swallow, I didn't need to add Giardia to my problems. The last thing I needed was a diarrhea inducing parasite.

After resting for about a half an hour, I decided to head up Sugar Mountain. I had not seen anyone for a few days now so I left my pack in the tent. There was no one around to steal it. My food was sealed in a "bear-proof" container, so nothing should have been able to smell it either. I got out my camera and headed up the trail.

The route was steep in places and soon I could feel my legs burning with exertion. I was glad I had left my pack behind. Unfortunately, I will have to retrace my steps tomorrow since this is the route I will be taking. Of course, I am going to have to do it with all of my equipment. I have to remember to make sure I stretch out well before starting off.

I made it to the top without incident. All around me was the beauty of nature. I set the camera for "panorama" and started clicking away. I had taken maybe a half dozen pictures when I heard voices. They were coming from the eastern portion of the Greenstone Ridge trail, which leads to Mount Desor. They were still far enough away to be indistinct, but they were getting closer. While I could not make out the words, I thought I could detect a note of panic in their tones.

Soon the voices, one low and one high, were close enough that I could make out at least one word out of every three. They were arguing about something; it sounded like which trail to take. The lower voice, which I assumed was male, wanted to keep "going forward." There was a distinct note of panic in his insistences. The other, higher, probably female voice, seemed to want to go back.

I was torn between slinking off back to my campsite and waiting where I stood. The Good Samaritan side wanted to stay and offer to help the couple find their way. I had one of my maps in my back pocket. The more selfish part wanted to slink back to my campsite and hope they did not come anywhere near it. The last thing I wanted to do was become embroiled in a lovers' quarrel.

I was still standing where the two trails met when my decision was made for me. The air was rent with a horrible scream.

The male hiker had spotted me and screamed.

A few embarrassing minutes later introductions had been made and I discovered why they were arguing. I will not try to recount the conversation verbatim, but the gist of it was that Stan and Cindy had been hiking for a few days. They had started at one end of the Greenback Ridge trail and were moving west to Windigo where they had made an appointment for the ferry to bring them back to Rock Harbor.

They were both avid outdoors-people. It was apparent from their gear that they spared no expense when it came to gadgets. They each had a high end GPS unit attached to their bags. The bags themselves were ultra-light and expensive looking, as was their clothing. I had no doubt that their tent would be able to withstand gale force winds but only weighed a few ounces.

Not that I was jealous or anything.

Among the gizmos which they had brought with them was an emergency radio. It was the kind which monitored the weather and national emergency stations and alarmed if anything was announced. They said when it went off they had expected to hear about a storm brewing on the lake. To their surprise, they heard the same thing repeated every five minutes.

"All citizens are advised to seek shelter immediately. Emergency shelters have been established at fire stations, foul weather shelters, and some schools. Tune into your local news broadcast for further details. If you are unable to reach a shelter, remain indoors with the doors and windows securely locked. Do not allow anyone in until given the All Clear by local authorities.

"The National Guard has been mobilized in some urban areas to assist with crowd control and disease containment. The CDC is currently researching the disease, but at this time they do not have a treatment. They have established quarantine areas in the worst hot zones. These quarantines are being enforced by the police and the National Guard. Anyone attempting to violate a quarantine area by either entering or leaving is subject to immediate arrest.

"Do not attempt to treat anyone showing signs of the disease. Avoid contaminated individuals at all costs, regardless of their age or relation to you. If you come in contact with an infected individual, report to the authorities immediately. Do not attempt to restrain infected individuals. Authorities have been sent to all areas of the outbreak to care for the infected.

"The infected display a number of symptoms including poor motor control, lack of higher cognitive function, slurred speech, and a grayish green pallor. Physicians assume that there is some form of nerve damage by the vector which causes infected individuals to appear impervious to pain. If you see anyone displaying any of these symptoms, or behaving erratically, err on the side of caution and inform your local authorities."

At least, that is what Stan said the broadcast said. I doubted that he could remember all of the announcement verbatim, even if he did listen to three repetitions of it. Of course, they could not get a signal on their radio for me to hear.

Their argument stemmed from their inability to decide what to do next. One of them, I am not really sure who was on which side, wanted to head back to Rock Harbor. There would be people there. This was also the port which has the most activity, so it was more likely to have someone with recent news. The other person wanted to press on to the Ranger Station at Windigo.

After more bickering amongst themselves, they turned to me for my opinion.

I told them that both sounded like good ideas and each had their merits. However, if they really wanted information, Windigo was their best bet. They could make it easily from where they stood.

I neglected to tell them that I was headed there myself tomorrow. Nor did I say that I was camped a short walk away. I assume that they saw that I did not have a pack and surmised that I was already set up for the night near the Ranger Station. They did not ask, and I did not divulge.

It was incredibly selfish of me, but I did not want to give up my last night of peace and quiet. Odds are they will still be in Windigo when I get there. The ferry is not due until the afternoon. We will have all morning to discuss the news of the larger world when I get there.

I admit, I am a little curious, but I am going to do my best to put it out of my head for now.

I wonder if Jan is alright.

PS. The sunset was brilliant. I think the batteries in my camera are just about dead.

Sept 12, 2009

08:45 a.m.

The sunrise was even more brilliant today than the sunset was last night, even if I am on the wrong side of the island for sunrises. This may be because this is likely my last moment of solitude. I prefer to think that it is due to the low clouds hanging overhead. The sun tinted their edges a brilliant pink while their centers remained gray.

If I remember my grade school meteorology correctly, the color of this morning's sky indicates that sailors should take warning. I assume this goes for people on an island in the middle of a lake large enough to be called a landlocked sea as well.

Although it was nice to have the time alone, I do not like the look of those clouds. I think it is probably a good thing that I am leaving today.

Time to pack everything up and head on up the trail.

Sept 12, 2009?
8:20 p.m.
Karma is a bitch.

I dragged my heels today, not wanting to spend the whole day in Windigo with Cindy and Stan. The hike itself was not bad, mostly downhill. Like the rest of the Greenridge trail, there are some areas where the trail is marked by rock cairns, some of which are easy to miss. I took it slow and managed not to miss any this time. When I was here with Jan we missed one of these turn offs and our hike ended up three times longer than we had intended.

I saw Stan and Cindy again, but not at Windigo. As before, they were bickering and I heard them coming up the trail near the Washington Creek Campground, less than a mile away from the Ranger Station.

Once again, I felt the urge to hide. This time I gave in to that urge.

"There is no one there!" Stan whined.

"Maybe the Ranger was sick."

"Even if he was sick, he would have come. Especially with all of the noise that we were making. There was no one there and there is always someone there on days when boats are due to arrive."

"Okay, fine." Cindy sounded exasperated. I could understand why. Stan's voice was starting to grate on my nerves.

"So what makes you think that there is going to be anyone at Rock Harbor? Maybe they all left. Maybe the boats aren't coming."

"Maybe they are waiting there for us with cake and ice cream. Either way, we won't know until we get there, so there is no use worrying about it now, is there?"

Stan's reply was unintelligible.

"Is there?" Cindy asked again.

"No, dear," Stan replied, utter defeat in his voice.

I waited off of the trail until I was sure that I would not be seen. Then I crept out. I watched my back trail for signs of the couple's return. Finally, I headed off the way they had come.

The trail was mostly downhill from here. I resisted the urge to jog down the trail. Although part of me wanted to reach the station and confirm the ferry's arrival, another part of me did not want to see the end to my solitude.

Perhaps Dr. Ross was right. Perhaps I just needed some time to reacquaint myself with myself in order to feel at ease without Jan. Perhaps all of the time alone in the woods had scrambled my brains. Psychobabble nonsense.

Of course, one has to be careful of what one wishes for. I was mourning the impending loss of solitude. I needn't have worried. I would have plenty of opportunities for more self-reflection.

The ranger station was abandoned.

It was also ransacked.

Someone, I assume Stan and/or Cindy, had emptied the display case of most of the consumables and that whoever had done so was not acting in any official capacity. The cabinets were not simply open, they were smashed. Jagged pieces of glass twinkled on the shelves which had held chocolate bars, packages of trail mix, and energy drinks.

The chalk board behind the desk announced the weather forecast, sunrise and sunset, and tide times for the 10th. No one had updated it in at least two days.

This worried me.

As Stan had said, someone was always there when a boat was due to arrive. At least, there was supposed to be someone there. I had a few hours to wait before the boat was due, so I went back out onto the low wooden porch and sat.

The longer I waited, the more anxious I got. Finally, knowing that the ferry was not due to arrive for hours, I walked down to the dock. From there I had a commanding view of Lake Superior and the sky overhead. The water was an ominous dark gray. The waves looked cold and menacing. The sky did not offer much in the way of hope. It, too, was gray, the gunmetal clouds hanging low.

Soon, it began to rain.

I had managed to go the whole trip without getting too wet, so it was inevitable that it should begin to pour while I was out of the wilderness and waiting for the ferry. The rain was cold and insistent. Soon I was soaked, despite my poncho. I toyed with the idea of heading back to the ranger station. Surely the boat captain would come ashore to look for his passenger.

But maybe not.

I waited on the dock.

I waited in the rain.

I waited until the ferry was hours overdue and the sun had sunk below the horizon. There was no spectacular sunset this evening. There was only a brief flare of orange where the clouds met the sea, then a more complete darkness.

The ferry had not come.

Had I gotten the days wrong? Was I early by a day? I could not have misjudged my time on the trail that by that much. Or was I late? Had I spent too much time on the trail and missed the ferry? Again, not possible.

No, I was certain of it. If nothing else, I had this journal to prove my internal calendar.

So I was at the dock at the right time on the right day, but the ferry was not there. If the mistake was not mine, it must have been the boat captain's.

So where did that leave me?

Sitting in the dark, in the rain, on the dock.

The Windigo campsite was not far off. It would be less than a half a mile, but it would mean hiking in the dark. It would also mean setting up in the dark and the rain. There was probably a shelter there. These were generally a sloped roof over a pallet with a screen door.

I opted instead to head back to the ranger station. Technically there was no camping at the station. I would be happy to get kicked out. That would mean that someone had shown up. Perhaps a ranger or other park official would have more of an idea of what was going on.

I looked around for a phone, or a radio of some kind. There was something in the back that looked like a CB, but it didn't work. I am going to grab something to eat, then try to find that little TV that the ranger was watching when I got here days ago.

Sept 12, 2009

10:15 p.m.

There is nothing here of any use. I can not find anything with which to contact the outside world, or even the other ranger station. The TV is useless. I think the storm, and it is a storm now, is messing with the signal. All I get is "Looking for signal" no matter what station I put it on.

I am gong to try and get some sleep. Maybe things will look better in the morning.

At least I have someplace dry.

SEPT 13, 2009

12:00 noon

The rain has let up a little today. It is vacillating between a fine mist and a steady drenching. I spent the morning sitting out on the docks, looking for the ferry. I have left my gear at the ranger station along with a note stating where I am.

I had to wait an extra day for the boat so the captain can damn well wait a few minutes for me to run up and grab my stuff.

SEPT 13, 2009

8:48 p.m.

No ferry, no rangers, no signs of anyone but me. My longed-for solitude has become something of a curse. I don't know if I should stay here and wait for someone to come pick me up or head back to the other side of the island. Maybe Stan and Cindy were right.

I am too tired to decide now. I will think about it in the morning.

SEPT 14, 2009

5:17 a.m.

Slept poorly. Storms were very loud. I alternated between trying to sleep, my head buried in my sleeping bag, and trying to get reception on the little television. I did manage to get in part of a news broadcast. I was able to watch about five minutes of a panel discussion between a doctor, someone in military uniform, and someone in a suit who was so smarmy that he must have been a politician. Unfortunately, I caught the end of the broadcast. Any actual discussion had ended long before I got the signal. All I was able to witness was discordant yelling. No information, other than something bad has happened somewhere and everyone is too busy blaming everyone else to actually do anything about it.

Perhaps it is a good thing that I am stuck here on the island. At least I am relatively safe from any contagions spread by inter-human contact.

Of course, the problem with staying here is that I am quickly running out of supplies. The gas canister for my little stove is almost empty. Not that it matters. I ate the last of the dehydrated meals last night for dinner. I have a few power bars and a handful of energy boost gel packs left. The bars make a decent, if small, meal. The gels are really just carbs in a foil package. They are good for a quick burst of energy, but will not sustain me long.

If only there was something left here at the station. I checked the back rooms last night. Nothing in the storeroom either. Stan and Cindy cleaned the place out completely.

I definitely can not stay here. There should be stores of food at Rock Harbor, but even the hotel may be low on supplies this late in the season. I wonder if there are any people who live on the island year round.

The big decision now is how to get there, via the Minong Ridge Trail or the Greenstone. Fortunately, they left me some maps and guidebooks.

Sept 14, 2009
12:35 p.m.

The hot shower I took before leaving Windigo was refreshing, but I would trade a week's worth of warm water for a good breakfast.

Both Minong and Greenstone should take anywhere from three to five days to hike. Minong runs along the north shore, so I would have a better chance of spotting passing boats. It is also the more difficult of the two. Greenstone should be a faster hike, so I opted for it.

Unfortunately, the first leg is mostly uphill. There is a lot of up and down and my thighs are burning. I have only stopped for a little while to catch my breath. If I want to make it to a campsite by dark, I will have to press on soon.

I can see the Canadian shoreline from here. It does not look as if anything horrible has happened. If everything is falling to pieces like the news seems to indicate (and what Stan said), then wouldn't I be able to tell?

Maybe not from this far away.

Maybe not at all.

Sept 14, 2009

9:55 p.m.

I am not sure exactly where I am. I know that I am on the far side of Mount Desor, but beyond that, I have no idea. Trying to push it was a mistake.

I started off the day climbing Sugar Mountain. I could have taken the side trail to the Island Mine campground, but I thought I could push forward and reach South Lake Desor.

The combination of all of the steep climbing and the lack of food has slowed me down immensely. The sun is now completely down. My flashlight beam is getting weaker. I should have grabbed batteries back at the ranger station.

The campground is near the lake, but I have not hit the lake yet. I am afraid to keep pushing forward for fear of losing the trail. It makes more sense to stop here for the night and start up again in the morning.

This is a breach of the contract that I signed stating that I would only camp in "designated areas." Of course, I also had a contract with the ferryman to pick me up. I know it is childish, but they broke their word first.

Besides, if everything is as bad as it seems, I guess sleeping on the trail is fairly small pickings.

There are two pieces of good news. One, at least it stopped raining. And two, I found another one of those bushes with the thimbleberries. Sounds like dinner to me.

Sept 15, 2009
   4:55 a.m.
There is enough sun to write by, so there is enough sun to walk by. If I start now I should be able to bypass South Desor for the next campground down the trail.

A quick stop for a breakfast of berries and I am off.

Sept 15, 2009
   1:28 p.m.
Those were not thimbleberries.

Sept 16, 2009
   4:45 p.m.
Whatever those berries were, I should not have eaten them. Two days of hiking, lost. I was forced to stop at South Desor after all. There I spent the better part of the last two days too sick to move. I still feel weak as water. I do not know if it is what I ate or what I have not eaten.

Regardless, I have to get moving soon. I am not going to get any stronger waiting around here. If only Stan and Cindy had left a little something. I could have been at Rock Harbor by now. I would not have had to eat those damn berries and been so sick.

Sept 17, 2009
   9:58 a.m.
I have reached the lookout tower which marks the halfway point between the last campground and the next. Normally I would rest here and have a bite to eat. There are no bites to be had and my stomach is

still sore from being ill. I am just pausing for a moment to catch my breath, then I will press on.

Sept 17, 2009
2:01 p.m
Hatchet Lake Campground. I should stop here, but there is still plenty of daylight left. I feel energized for some reason. Continuing on, despite common sense which tells me to stop.

Sept 17, 2009
11:47 p.m.
Definitely should have stopped at Hatchet Lake.

Sept 18, 2009
07:28 a.m.
Another cold, hungry morning. I managed to get much farther than I have ever done before, doubt that I will be able to do it again, but I am strangely surprised at my abilities. I pushed further than I would have thought possible.

Dr. Ross was right, I have learned a lot about myself on this trip.

I traversed two mountains yesterday. Normally one would have taxed me. I am so hungry and tired.

Last night I camped at Chickenbone West.

I know that there is another campground a little further down the trail. I know that I can make it at least that far.

Last night I thought I heard something as I was setting up camp. There is no way that I could have heard what I thought I did, especially if they are at the next camping site.

I could have sworn that I heard the arguing of that abhorrent couple of food thieves.

I will find out soon enough.

What have I done?

I swear I did not mean to,
I would never. It was an accident.
I was just so mad and he kept lying and the wood was right there.

Date and Time Unknown

Although I shudder to write this, I feel that it is in my best interest to record the horrible things that have transpired since my last entry. Perhaps the writing of it will give me clarity.

The sounds that I had heard that night were indeed Stan and Cindy. They had been camping at Chickenbone East for a few days. They were prevented from getting any further, despite their two day lead, because of Stan's injury. He fell or slipped or something, I did not quite follow the story. The result was a leg which was swollen and dark. The skin was mottled and foul smelling.

I did not like the look of that leg.

I had not planned to confront them. I had not planned to do anything at all. When I reached their campsite, Cindy came running towards me. She asked for a first-aid kit, then for food.

Something happened to me then.

I began screaming at them, accusing them of stealing all of the food from the ranger station. I asked why they didn't leave anything for me, why they didn't have anything left for themselves, and what had happened to all of the stores.

They denied taking anything. They said that the ranger station had been ransacked when they got there. Cindy said that was why they did not stay there.

I did not believe them.

I demanded that they share with me whatever they had taken from the station.

I do not know what happened next, or in what order.

I remember Stan's whining denials and threatening him with a piece of the firewood that they had collected.

Cindy was very quiet while Stan and I argued.

I remember Cindy screaming.

The next thing I can recall clearly is looking down at the bloodied chunk of wood I held in my hand. The first thing that went through my head as I stared at the clumps of hair and tissue which dotted its length was that this was fresh wood. It was strong and sturdy. Firewood was supposed to be limited to what hikers found, "down and dead."

Someone had been breaking the rules.

Stan was lying there, practically in the fire ring. His features were unrecognizable from the shoulders up. His head and face were a pulpy mess of red and gray with little bits of hair and exposed bone.

Cindy was nowhere to be found.

All of the frustration, all of the anger, which had been welling up inside me, rushed out in a horrible, murderous flood. It was not just the ferry and the hunger. It was Janice and the loneliness and everything else which had gone wrong in the last eighteen months. It all spilled over and I killed Stan.

I killed Stan.

And I was so hungry.

It would have been a crime to let all of that good meat go to waste.

I ate what I could. I left the purplish, injured limb alone.

I did not like the look of that leg.

Later, night.

I do not know how long I have been here. Has it been one day or many? Has it been a week?

Stan is gone, at least the edible portion of him.

But Cindy is still out there somewhere.

I thought I heard her rustling around in the bushes last night. I ran out after her, whether to assault or apologize I do not know.

I tore down the path towards the sound. I almost ran headlong into the dark shape which stood there, half on the trail, half off.

I would not have believed it if I had not seen it myself. Of course, I did not have my camera.

A pair of yellow eyes gleamed at me out of the darkness. The dark, dog-like-but-not, shape could have only been one thing.

The wolf did not attack, nor did it run away. It stared at me coolly, appraisingly, measuring me. Then, as if it recognized something in me, it turned and calmly walked away.

I WILL LOOK for Cindy in the morning. If I find her, I will stay here for a few more days. If I do not, I will assume that she has followed her original plan and headed off to the east and Rock Harbor. It will be difficult going for her without food or supplies, but she will be traveling light. Perhaps she will make it, perhaps not.

I might meet up with her on the trail and find her, tired, weak, injured like Stan.

Rock Harbor is definitely the correct destination. There will be more supplies, maybe food. And if not...at least there will be more people.

BRAINS

"The frontal lobe, the temporal lobe, and the parietal lobe are all part of what physical structure?"

"Brains."

"Very good, can anyone tell me what an EEG takes images of?"

"Brains."

"Correct. Neurons and glial cells are found where in the human body?"

"Brains."

"Excellent. What is the largest organ in the human body?"

"Brains."

Mr. Feldstein shook his head.

"No, I am sorry. The correct answer is skin."

Feldstein looked out over the class. Their milk white eyes stared back at him. Their grayish flesh was beginning to putrefy. Some areas, especially around the restraints, were decaying to a black liquid. That might become a problem.

The smell was definitely a problem. He sprayed the air around his desk with a liberal dose of disinfectant.

Yes, the smell and rot were problems. Of course, he could not get too close to them either. Tommy Comstock had tried to take a bite out of him just the other morning. He always had ben a trouble maker.

Still, three out of four answers correct. His students were better as zombies than the had ever been when they were alive.

Now if he could only get them to raise their hands.

GRANDPA

Blue-green algae spread across a cheek
    once the landing place of thousands of tiny kisses
    Milk blank stare, these windows to the soul
    forever shuttered, eyes which had once looked upon
    every act as a miraculous accomplishment.
    Lips blackened, rotted through, teeth
    which once smiled
    now bared
    grimace not grin
    closer, ever closer
    leaning in, not to praise nor kiss,
    but to bite.

THE CORPSE
A HAIKU

Rancid, flyblown,
   putrified, decaying,
   moldering,
   decomposing
   carious

yummy.

BEAUTY REDEFINED

An expanse of beauty extends before my eyes
    Unlike the fields of my youth.
    I recall the green paddocks
    the bright spots of color screaming for attention
    demanding my view.
    Before.
    When we would celebrate life
    in all its glory and fleeting fragility.
    Before.
    When the line between death and life is no longer solid
    beauty takes on new meaning
    and the eye is attracted to that which it once would have shunned.
    The field below, carpeted with the dead.
    Flyblown bodies baking in the sun.
    Corpses which lie still
    which do not rise.
    An expanse of beauty extends before my eyes.

GREETINGS OF THE SEASON

GREETINGS OF THE SEASON,

Right off the bat let me apologize for the generic letter. I would dearly love to send a personal note to each and every one of you, but everything has been so hectic here at Casa del Taylore that there just isn't time. Between sending out the cards, preparing the blood sacrifices, and shopping, shopping, shopping I barely have time to enjoy the whimpers and screams coming from the dungeon. Of course, it is the holiday season so we have to make time for the things which are important to us and for me this means family. It comes down to short but personal handwritten notes or lots of copies of the same letter. You'll all have to excuse that I chose option two.

Speaking of family, it has been another up and down year for the Taylore and the Bihn families. I'm sure you all remember the 'excitement' we had at the end of last year. I'm also sure you've all heard the good news, but just in case you were hiding in a cave, Billy got let out on a technicality. It's funny how crucial evidence can just go missing sometimes (thank for the help with the casting Grandma Bihn). Billy, I'm sorry -- William Earving Taylore, what law states that once you kill more than three people the police and the press have to start referring to you by the most formal version of your name?

Anyway, Billy decided that the first thing he wanted to do is come back to the old homestead. Bless his soul, he always was about as smart as a bag of tacks but not as sharp. It was lovely to have him home for a while but he couldn't stay. He simply brought too much scrutiny along with him. The Sheriff was certain that he had done what he was accused of. There was even rumor that he had something to do with the witnesses disappearances, although how he could have done that from a jail cell is a stone mystery.

We all know he just wasn't that powerful. His daddy may have been able to do it, Grandpa Taylore for sure, but not Billy.

Well we just couldn't convince Billy that he couldn't stay so we did what we had to do for the good of the family. We do what we must. Augustine did it nice and public, made it look like someone trying to get retribution for what Billy'd done. I understand the Sheriff is looking at the daddy of one of the victims as a suspect. This makes Billy's widow happy.

If you have a keen eye you will notice that Billy isn't the only one missing from this year's family portrait. We lost one of our favorite scullions this spring. I think her given name was Jeanie or Joaney. We all called her Red, on account of that beautiful long hair of hers. I told Terry that the southern point of that pentagram was too close to where Red's chains were anchored but he went ahead and did the summoning anyway. You can't tell some men anything. We gained a new familiar but lost someone who had been with the family for nearly a decade. You have to take the bitter with the sweet.

I still remember the day when we picked her up at that rest area, it seems like yesterday. It just is not as easy to acquire people like her any more. We have already picked up a replacement. You can see him cowering there in the picture behind Uncle Liam. So far, we're not all that impressed. I'm hoping that he will come around soon. If not, there will be fresh winter sausage on the feast table.

The year was not all losses. We had our fair share of additions, too. Athgoal, the familiar that Terry raised is taking to the training real well. It's already housebroken and is accepting commands from everyone on the Bihn side of the family. It's like Grandma Bihn always said "a steady mind and a firm hand are all you need to train a dog or a demon."

The family's big news was the birth of the twins - Stephen and Marcus. Lacie's two beautiful boys, well, one and a half beautiful boys, were born this spring and they are already scooting around like you wouldn't believe. Those boys are going to be a handful for sure. Two heads are better than one, but I have a feeling the twins are going to have to be home schooled.

Other than that is has been a pretty uneventful year. Just the usual--caring for the crops, appeasing the Elder Ones, making sure the righteous townsfolk don't get too upity.

Speaking of Elder Ones there is still a lot of work to be done before the Feast so I had better cut this short. Hopefully these cards will get to you all on time. Wishing you the best of all the worlds, from our family to yours -- Happy Holidays!

Love,
Mae Belle Taylore (nee Bihn)

THE STAIRWELL

I

I was so lonely and scared. Perhaps it was selfish of me to have returned, but where else would I go? Where else but this little house on the shore of Lake Huron? This was the only place I had ever known real love. I never meant for anyone to get hurt, at least, not at first.

II

Her screams when she first saw me pierced right through me. Of course, everything goes right through you when you are non-corporeal, but you know what I mean.

I don't know what I expected, but it wasn't screams.

That's a lie. I know exactly what I expected. I thought she would see me and burst into tears of joy. I thought she would rush to me, arms open, only to stop a few steps away. Melancholy would wash over her features. I would tell her that our love would be different now but the sheer fact that I was there was testament to the power of our connection. Even the grave and all that.

Yes, I had a little speech prepared.

So you can see why it was so painful when instead of tears and cries of love I was met with shrieks of terror.

Time. She just needs a little time to adjust to the idea.

III

APPARENTLY NOT.

The problem isn't a matter of adjusting to the idea of my return. It's that she doesn't even know who I am. As if she has hundreds of other lovers who would defy death to be with her. Maybe she does have someone else. Maybe she has already forgotten about me, moved on, found comfort in the warm arms of someone whose heart still beats.

She did seem rather enraptured by that tool from the cable show. Maybe she was impressed that he had come all the way from Los Angeles to our two stoplight rural Michigan town. Maybe I was just being jealous.

Again, I never meant for anyone to get hurt. Really, what do you expect when you run around in the dark with night vision goggles on rather than turning on the lights?

Who watches these programs anyway? Does anyone really believe two idiots weighed down with flashy equipment being trailed by cameramen weighed down by less equipment?

At first it was kind of funny. I was leaning against the wall at the end of the upstairs hallway while they were slowly walking up the stairs. The one with the beard was staring intently at the little flashy thing in his hand. The other one maintained a constant monologue for the cameraman trailing behind. Some nonsense about the history of the house which bore no resemblance to anything which had ever happened here.

They were three quarters of the way up the stairs, still a good fifteen feet from where I was, when the tool with all of the tools stopped short. I'm sure the well crafted panic on his face played well in the green not-light of the night vision cam.

THE STAIRWELL

"Did you hear that?" Fake fear made his voice rise.

"What was that?" His partner was almost trembling. I smelled Emmy.

"It was the echo of your own big feet," I hollered. Of course they could not hear me.

"It's cold. Yes, we have definitely entered a cold spot."

They were whispering now. but loud enough for the next door neighbors to hear. I approached them in spite of myself. They were both shivering. I don't know if it was supposed to be from the cold or from fear. I was sure the camera was capturing it, either way.

"Spirit of the staircase, we mean you no harm."

They crept a few steps higher.

"We are simply scientists seeking knowledge."

The little gizmo in the bearded guy held started to emit a droning sound which rose in pitch as he climbed the stairs. Was there something to their crazy equipment after all? He pointed the thingamabob at me and the tone dropped noticeably. He swung it in a wide arc. When it was pointed towards the other end of the hall it started to whistle.

Both men turned their backs to me and addressed the empty hallway.

"If you are there, can you give us some sort of sign?"

I stared at them for a moment. I felt the urge as a little tickle in the back of my mind. It was that same feeling I used to get when I was a child. My grandmother said it was the devil on my shoulder, prodding me on.

I could blame the two goofballs with their flashing lights and beeps and whirls. They were asking for it. Literally, they were asking me to give them a sign. Maybe something in the way they asked compelled me to do what I did. Then that part wouldn't be my fault. Still, it wouldn't explain when happened later.

Whatever the reason, demands of the inquisitive, naughty urges, or just plain meanness on my part, I glided forward until I was just inches from the two of them.

Then I manifested.

I wish I could adequately describe the process. It's not as if I was a wispy nothing in the air one minute and something, if not solid at least opaque the next. It was something I had to concentrate on. There is a squeezing feeling, which I supposed I should not have since I don't have a body anymore. The only comparison I can think of is a little vulgar.

It's kind of like when you have to belch.

When you really need to belch.

You know, when you have that dull pain in the center of your chest and you know that if you focus on it just right you can get rid of it? I bet you do. I bet if I asked you to tell me what you do to get rid of that feeling you wouldn't be able to tell me. Sure, you swallow, but then what? Is there a muscle or three involved? What is it that you tense, or relax, or whatever?

Well, it's like that. I concentrated or focused or whatever it was that I did. I felt the air swirling around me. I mean, I actually <u>felt</u> the air. It tingled like static electricity. I felt myself getting heavier. I was, somehow, more than I had been.

It took the two geeks a couple of seconds to notice me. The host guy, the one who talked a lot, noticed first.

"As our regular viewers now, a sudden drop in aggregate temperature, localized to one geographic area, is a common factor in many hauntings. We call this a cold spot…"

He turned his head a bit, caught a glimpse of me, and stopped. For the first time that night, he was silent. His eyes widened. I tried to smile, but by that point I was so ticked off I'm not sure that I managed it. In fact, I'm not really sure what I look like when I try to go solid. The first time I did it was for her and it made her scream. This time the reaction was pretty similar.

Talking Guy, now Not Talking Guy, grabbed Bearded Guy's shoulder. Bearded Guy spun, took one look at me, and screamed like a small child.

I'm not sure what made me do it, but I leaned in and said "boo."

I don't know if they heard me. I don't know if they even really saw me. I do know that Bearded Guy dropped the little whatsit and ran. It stopped beeping and flashing the second it was out of his hand. It hit the floor with a dull thud.

By that point they were already halfway down the stairs. I watched them from the landing.

I did not follow them. No matter what they may have said later, I did not chase them down the stairs.

I was still at the top of the stairs when the Bearded Guy's foot slipped. He reached out for the railing. His hand went between two of the carved wooden uprights and stayed there as his body continued forward. There was a snapping sound followed by another scream. He slid down the rest of the stairs on his backside. His right arm was bent funny and in the wrong place. He looked like he had a second elbow. The hand swung uselessly from his already swelling wrist.

Talking Guy didn't fare much better. When Bearded Guy slipped, his partner almost crashed into him. To avoid contact he jumped. As the banister snapped Bearded Guy's wrist, Talking Guy leapt over him. He missed him completely. He landed on the stairs with both feet, three steps below his partner. It was just like something out of the movies.

Of course, in the movies he would have kept his feet under him. Instead he pitched forward and slammed face first into the newel post at the bottom of the stairs. I could hear the crunch from where I stood. Blood gushed. It did not stop him. Talking Guy picked himself up and kept running, down the hall, out the door, and into the night without so much as a backward glance to see if Bearded Guy or any of the crew was following.

IV

You would think that would have been it, right? I know I did. I had come to the sad conclusion that she was not happy to see me and really did not want me there. If I knew how to leave I would have, but I didn't. So I made up my mind to "live and let live" if that can be said about the dead.

When she came upstairs, I went downstairs. I made sure to stay as far away from her as I could. No "localized temperature changes." No attempts to talk to her. No attempts to touch her.

I watched, but from a distance

I resigned myself to being an unseen, unheard, and ultimately unimportant part of her life.

Every day I felt smaller, less than I had the day before. Maybe if I stopped concentrating on being near her I would just disappear. I told myself that each glimpse of her would be the last. If I could only let go…

But the project wasn't moving along quickly enough for her.

I was upstairs again when the door opened. That back corner of the hallway seemed to be where I ended up when I wasn't concentrating on being somewhere else. It was my default setting I guess.

I heard the outside door open. For a change, I was able to force myself not to steal a glance at her. The door closed. There was the rustle of people moving about, coats being removed and stored in the closet by the door.

People.

Plural.

She was talking to someone. That someone was answering back. His voice was low. Quiet low, but also register low.

She had brought another man into our house.

I could not make out much of what they were saying. He seemed to be trying to convince her of something. I heard the plaintive tone of her words, but not the words themselves. I distinctly heard the reply.

"It's for the best. If it is him, don't you want him to be at peace?"

She said something else and he replied.

"No, it's best if you don't watch. Maybe you should wait in the kitchen."

She said something else and he answered. I heard a door open, the coat rustle again, and then another door open and close.

She had left.

Left me alone in the house with a strange man.

I looked over the railing. The man in question was dressed all in black. He was hunched over a bag, his back to me. He pulled what looked like a scarf out of the bag, kissed it, and slipped it over his head.

THE STAIRWELL

I knew what he was before he turned around. I had a pretty good idea who he was, too.

The black robed man started up the stairs, bag in one hand, Bible in the other.

Father O'Flanagan.

I turned to leave. I hadn't cared for the man and his heavy handed, fire and brimstone preaching when I'd been alive. I certainly wasn't going to listen to him now that I wasn't.

I couldn't glide.

For the first time since I had come back to the house, I could not simple glide across the floor. I tried to will myself into the bedroom and failed. I was rooted to the spot.

Father O'Flanagan continued his slow ascent. He was chanting something in Latin. I took a bit of the language back when I was in school. We all had to. What he was saying now made no sense to me. It didn't sound like words at all. It was more of a buzzing sound that wormed its way into my head.

The priest's voice rose. The buzzing sound turned into a skull splitting shriek. I tried to clap my hands to my ears, but of course I had no hands, ears, nor skull. A dull ache started in what I thought of as my chest.

O'Flanagan was at the top of the stairs now. He turned his head to the right, to the left, then back to the right. He continued towards me. He could not see me, but he was walking right towards me. The ache at my core had bloomed into a fiery pain.

He could not see me. That was it! Maybe if I could make him see me I could scare him off like the others. I did my best to ignore the pain and the buzz-saw whine and focused on materializing. At first, I could not even remember how I had done it before.

I heard a gasp and knew that I had managed something. Father O'Flanagan stopped his chanting. It was just a moment, but that moment without pain gave me the clarity to focus.

I revealed myself to him. I willed myself to be as frightening as possible.

O'Flanagan dropped the bag. He started chanting again. He held the Bible up before him like a shield. His right hand slipped into his pocket. It came out with a small silver flask.

I wanted to make a wry comment about needing a drink. I wanted to try the "boo" again. The agony in my center prevented me from doing anything coherent. I shrieked. It was the sound of anger and pain wrapped around each other.

I'm pretty sure he heard me.

The top of the flask flipped open. He snapped his wrist and the contents splashed out. They hit me and I felt them. It burned. The new pain broke whatever had been holding me in place. I ran forward. I did not glide or slip, I ran. I was more substantial than I had been since death.

I don't think the good Father was expecting that.

I ran forward and slapped the flask from his hand. It spiraled over he railing and hit the first floor hallway. He shouted something at me. It wasn't Latin or English. I think he was cursing me in his native tongue.

I reached out and grabbed him. I was moving too fast; I was too angry to be amazed by the fact that I could actually touch him. Touch him I did. I grabbed him by the vestments and lifted him over my head. I held him there for a moment. For one brief second he hung there.

Then I pitched him over the railing.

His head and shoulders hit the small table by the stairs, the one we always put the day's mail on. There was a small vase there holding a single flower. The vase shot off and plummeted to the floor. It shattered into tiny blue shards. The table splintered under O'Flanagan's weight. He hit the floor among shards of glass and wood. The flower was no where to be seen.

The pain stopped. It didn't wane, it simply vanished. I stared down and the unmoving corpse of the priest. I knew he was dead. The mad jumble of limbs and the awkward angle of his neck made that clear.

V

I don't know why I didn't think of this before.

Sometimes the answer won't come one it's own. Sometimes you have to be shocked by something so abnormal, so unusual, that the friction of that thought sparks other ideas.

As I stared down at the dead priest I came to a realization. I would never be what she wanted me to be. I would never be flesh and blood again. I would never be able to wrap my arms around her and hold her. Our love would never be more than a shadow of what it had once been.

I can never again be like her.

Soon she will return home. She will horrified by what she finds. She may run out of the house. She may even stay away for a while.

Yet she will come back. At some point she will return to our house. She will climb the stairs to her bedroom.

I can never again be like her.

But she can be like me.

I will tell her that our love will be different now. I will tell her that not even death can separate us.

It will be death that brings us together at last.

DIGITAL MEDIA

"Wake him."

The body lay slumped in the chair. Its head lolled back and to one side. One of the men stepped out of the shadows. A vicious slap to the face did nothing. A bucket of cold water was fetched and dumped on the supine figure. It came to life with a sputter. The man, now fully awake, struggled briefly against the bonds which held him to the chair.

After he a moment, he slumped. His head hung forward. The light from the bare bulb overhead illuminated the man's bald pate.

"Look at me," the voice said.

The man in the chair sobbed once. His chin remained tucked against his chest, either to avoid seeing the surroundings or as a defensive posture.

"Head up, Sunshine." The words seemed warm, but the voice was as cold and dark as the inky blackness which surrounded the small circle of light.

The man in the chair raised his head, his eyes squeezed shut. His eyes were so tightly closed that his whole face was a mass of wrinkles threatening to collapse in on itself.

"Open those eyes," the voice said. "Remember, you asked for this."

"I never..." the man in the chair started to protest. A hand shot into the feeble light and caught him, open handed, along his jaw. His head snapped back, his teeth clacking shut audibly.

"Do not contradict me, Mr. Johnson. You not only asked for this, you paid for it. In fact," there was a rustling of papers, "you requested it seventeen times."

"But I, I didn't..."

"No, of course you didn't." The voice had moved slightly. Johnson, the man in the chair, thought it was coming from his left side. He turned his head to follow it, but he could see nothing outside of the light bulb's illumination.

"Where am I?" he asked. He did not remember anything beyond leaving his office that evening. Yesterday evening? He was not even sure of the time. From where he sat the room he was in was utterly featureless. The darkness could have hidden a warehouse, an airport hanger, or a closet sized kitchenette. His whole world was defined by what he could see, what was directly below the bulb. Existence was reduced to his own body, naked except for brightly striped boxer shorts, and the chair to which he was bound. The chair was wooden, sturdy, with wide set legs. His arms were bound at wrist and elbow to its wide armrests. Other straps which felt like leather bit into his legs, chest, and waist. That was everything. That was his reality. A chair, some leather straps, and the ridiculous boxers he wished he had not worn.

That and the voice.

"Do you think that rules are important?"

The voice was definitely coming from the left side of the chair now. That seemed to fit, as the question was straight out of left field. Johnson did not know how to answer it.

"Um, rules?"

"Yes, Mr. Johnson, rules. Do you think that rules are important?"

"Sure, some rules. Others...I don't know."

"An honest answer, therefore a good answer." The voice continued to move, behind him now. Johnson tried to turn to follow it, but the high back of the chair stilled his head.

"I think that rules are important. They are necessary, essential.

Without rules, all would be chaos. Rules are imperative for the existence of modern society."

The voice was coming from directly behind them.

"Laws, on the other hand, can be corrupted. They tend to serve the strong, the powerful, to the exclusion of the weak and powerless. Good laws are based upon accepted rules. As such, if one follows the rules, one is safe. Do you agree Mr. Johnson?"

"Yeah, right. Rules are important." He whipped his head from side to side. He craned it to the right, but still could not make out the source of the voice.

"I am glad you agree."

The voice paused. In the silence which followed, Johnson thought that he could detect movement at the edges of the circle of light. Were there others in the room?

"The application of rules allows us to chart our way through life. They define what is permitted and what is proscribed. Of course, there is a dark side to the application of rules. It allows us to punish behavior which breaks the rules."

There was a scraping sound directly behind the chair. Johnson felt something grab his hair tightly. His head was slammed into the chair back.

"I am glad that you understand the importance of rules, Mr. Johnson." The voice whispered into his ear. Johnson could feel the warm breath on his cheek. "Now pay very close attention. I am going to tell you the rules of the most important game of your life. Are you listening closely?"

A squeak slipped from Johnson's throat. He nodded as best as he could with the hand twisted tightly in his hair.

"Good. Very good."

The grip on his hair relaxed. The voice began moving again.

"We are going to engage in a game somewhere between Jeopardy and Truth or Dare. The questions may be hard to answer, but I guarantee you will know the answers. There is only one topic -- your life. You must answer truthfully. There is no "Dare" option. You must also answer correctly."

The pacing stopped. The voice was off to his right. Johnson did not turn his head.

"You are right handed, correct?"

Johnson nodded.

"For the sake of clarity, please verbalize all of your answers."

"Yes, I am right handed."

"Good, very good. Your answers should be as succinct as possible, yes or no where possible. Do you understand?"

"Yes."

"Good. The rules state that you must answer every question. Now it is very important to remember, you must answer truthfully and you must answer correctly."

The voice had continued to move until it was directly in front of him again. Johnson peered into the darkness. His gaze was centered on where he assumed the owner of the voice was standing.

"Which is more important, honesty or intelligence?"

"Um, I am not sure. They are both…"

The voice cut him off.

"Don't worry. We have not started the game yet. I am just interested in your opinion on the matter. Let me phrase it a different way. Which is more abhorrent, someone who is wrong, or someone who deliberately lies?"

Johnson's throat dried up. He rasped out his answer.

"Lying is worse."

"We agree. It is far better to be incorrect then deliberately deceitful. So, we come to the final rules of the game, the rules regarding punishment. If you answer a question incorrectly, you will lose a finger on your left hand. You did not answer a question correctly. However, if you do know the answer and provide one which you know to be false, you will lose a finger from your right hand."

Johnson sobbed quietly.

"Now remember, the rules state that you must answer every question. Failure to answer will be considered a lie of omission and will result in the same punishment as a spoken lie. If you are not sure about an answer, it is better to guess. If you are wrong, you will only lose part of your left hand.

"Bear in mind, by answering you at least have the possibility of providing a correct answer. Failure to answer is a wrong answer assured. It is better to chance an educated guess, just like the SATs."

There was a slow scraping sound, like metal being drawn over stone. Johnson looked up. A long cruel looking knife gleamed in the light. The hand that held it was encased in a blue glove made of latex or rubber. The blade rose slowly until it was pointed at Johnson's right eye. He pulled his head back as far as the chair would let him.

"Twenty questions, Mr. Johnson. You have only to answer twenty questions. Of course, if you run out of fingers the game is over. Then we have to move to other parts."

Johnson turned his head, pressing it into the seat back.

"Let's begin."

"How long have you lived at your current address?"

Johnson blinked. Was that really one of the twenty questions? Were they really going to be that easy?

How accurate did he have to be? Johnson squeezed his eyes closed. He had moved in the fall a few years ago. It had been after he had gotten his new job. He was due for a five year pay bump next month…

"Your answer please."

"I have lived there for four years, ten months…"

He was stopped by a chuckle.

"There is no need to be that specific. Four years will suffice. I would have also accepted 'almost five years.' Don't worry about these first few questions, they are easy. If I need you to be precise, I will let you know."

The voice was sounded relaxed, almost charming.

"How long have you lived alone?"

The voice did not ask for precision, but in this case it would be easy to provide. He could answer down to the minute, if he knew the current date and time.

"About 18 months."

"And before that?"

Was that a question?

"Um, before that I was living with someone, Linda. She, she left."

"Yes, she did. How long has it been since you have been on a date?"

"A date?"

"Answering a question with a question is a stall tactic often used by people who are about fabricate their answer. Think very carefully about what you want your answer to be. How long has it been since you have been on a date?"

"I haven't really dated anyone. I don't go out."

Silence.

"Do you have to go out to be on a date?"

Seconds ticked by, then the realization hit him.

"Well, on-line dating. I have dated in Virtual World, the on-line …" his voice trailed off.

"So you have dated."

Statement, not one of the questions. Johnson swallowed hard.

"So the answer you provided was incorrect."

The voice came from his left side.

"No, wait! I did not understand the question!"

There was a flash of pain. Johnson looked down in time to see the knife blade, bloodied, no longer gleaming, retreat from the light. Then a burning pain shot through his arm. Blood spurted from his left hand. His little finger ended at the first knuckle. He strained forward in the chair. On the ground was a growing puddle of his blood. At the edge of it sat the other two thirds of his finger.

He opened his mouth to scream. He passed out instead.

This time it took more than water to bring him around.

The man in the chair opened his eyes just in time to see a slim figure retreat from the light. There was a stinging sensation in the crook of his right arm. He looked down and saw a single orb of blood nestled there. As he watched the orb swelled and burst. The trickle of blood ran across his arm. Its source was a tiny puncture in his vein.

He had a brief moment to wonder what he had been injected with before the throbbing started. With the throbbing came the memory.

A quick glance at his ruined left hand confirmed it. A bloody lump of gauze was taped to the side of his hand. He lifted his hand as much as the bindings would allow. It came away from the arm of the chair with a sticky wet sound.

He started screaming again.

There were no words. His shriek was the raw sound of panic, fear, and disbelief. It lasted until he ran out of breath. He drew a ragged breath, filling his lungs before beginning again.

Before he could, a hand connected with his cheek. It was much harder than the previous slap. The hand seemed different, too. It was harder, stronger.

"Mr. Johnson, if we could continue. We still have a lot of questions to go."

The voice was coming from the left side. The slap had been from the right. There were at least two different people in the room with him.

"Now, we have established that you 'date' in various on-line scenarios. We will return to that in a moment. What other internet activities do you perform?"

"The same as everyone else, I guess." Johnson did not know what the voice was looking for, but did not hesitate to answer. "E-mail, look up stuff, pay bills, surf the net."

"And when you surf the net, what do you look at?"

"All kinds of stuff. The usual stuff. What everyone looks at."

There was a glint of steel and a blaze of pain. The flat of the knife blade rapped down on the stump where Johnson's finger had been. Pain lanced up his arm. He felt the blood begin to flow again, pooling on the arm rest before dripping to the floor. He stifled another scream.

"A non-answer. Tread carefully, Mr. Johnson. You are perilously close to a lie of omission."

Johnson gulped air. The pain subsided to a throb. Each beat of his heart fueled the suffering. He closed his eyes for a moment and concentrated on his breathing.

"Better now?" the voice asked. "Good. Then I ask you again, what do you look at when you surf the net?"

"Amazon," Johnson blurted. "I buy books all of the time. I go to my bank's website. I… I look stuff up, you know, videos, cartoons, funny stuff. I watch movie trailers. I read the news. Sometimes I watch old episodes of TV shows."

"What else?"

"I don't know what else. Honest I don't."

His voice climbed higher, whining, pleading. The knife appeared again. The tip grazed his left arm. It was dragged gently up the arm to his shoulder. It was the faintest of touches, but the throbbing turned it to agony. The knife was sharp enough that the faint scratch was enough to draw a line of blood the length of his arm.

"What else do you use your computer for?"

An image popped into Johnson's mind. He opened his mouth to speak, but no words came forth.

"Tick, tock."

The man in the chair shook his head. He had an answer. He was unwilling to answer. It was too horrible. He would not admit to it. There was no way they could know.

He saw movement to his right. He tried to pull away, momentarily forgetting the leather straps. His hand slipped forward and tightened on the edge of the arm rest.

He felt the knife bite into the meat at the side of his hand. Johnson gripped the chair harder. His exhalation was more surprise than pain. He felt the blade slide away. It returned, bringing fresh agony with it. He watched in horror as the little finger on his right hand was replaced by the knife. Blood gushed over the blade which was wedged partially in the arm rest, partially in his hand. The tip had nicked his ring finger. His pinkie was gone at the base.

"What?" Johnson screamed. "What do you want you dirty, mother…"

What he could see of the room dimmed. The circle of light he sat in seemed to shrink. The edges of his vision became gray. He shook his head to clear it.

When his sight cleared, he saw that his right hand had been roughly bandaged. He did not remember anyone coming close enough to wrap the gauze around it. Had he passed out after all.

"Typing has now become significantly more difficult for you," the voice said in a mocking tone. "Before it becomes even harder for you to operate your computer, why don't you tell me what else you use it for."

"Chatting," said the man in the chair. "Instant messaging, chat rooms, all of that."

Johnson slumped in the chair. Even his voice sounded drained.

"And who do you chat with Mr. Johnson?"

He wanted to say "friends." He wanted to say "family."

Instead, he answered truthfully.

"People like me."

"And what does that mean, exactly?"

"People who … collect things."

"What sort of things?"

"Pictures."

The voice remained silent.

"Trophies."

No response.

"Bodies."

"Excellent."

"I'll tell you everything. I'll give you names. Please, just, no more. Please."

"How long?"

"How long what?"

Movement, pressure. The knife was poised for another cut. It rested on the ring finger of his right hand.

"You said people like you. How long have you been like you?"

"I don't, honestly, I don't know. I never …"

The knife blade made a quick down and to the side movement, a Benihana chef's movement. The finger spun away into the darkness.

"This is becoming tiring. When was the first time you visited the website?"

The man in the chair did not have to ask which website. The pain provided clarity.

"I read about it on-line, in a thread on another website I frequent."

The words were pouring out of him, gushing forth like the crimson pumping from his ruined right hand.

"I think it was a couple of years ago. At first I only looked at the welcome page. I was too scared to put in my credit card number so I did not sign up. I just looked at the pictures on the first page."

The knife came down again, severing the two remaining fingers of Johnson's right hand. As the blade descended, there was a squeak and a curse. The voice, or whoever was employing the knife, slipped in the blood puddled around the chair. As a result, the knife did not land as planned. The third finger was detached cleanly, but the index finger was not. Instead of hitting the joint, the sharp edged steel lodged in the bone between the hand and the first knuckle.

Metacarpal, thought Johnson as he screamed. The tunnel vision returned.

Someone through a towel at the man in the chair. The blue gloved hand shoved it onto the wound with a savage thrust. The pain cleared Johnson's mind.

"You got lucky, that time." The voice sounded ragged. The labored breathing could have been caused by anger or exertion.

"Lucky," Johnson repeated. He meant it to sound sarcastic, but the accompanying laugh held a tinge of mania.

"Yes, lucky. Your IP information is on record. You visited the site for the first time just under a year and a half ago. You watched one portion of one video, then signed up. You provided false information, but a correct credit card number. You spent over an hour on the site that same day.

"That was a deliberate lie and a lie of omission. The should have cost you two fingers. Maybe you will still be able to point when we are done here. That depends on you and your answers."

"Fuck you."

"I didn't think I was your type. However, while we are on the subject, what is your type, Mr. Johnson? What was that first video that enticed you to join the website?"

"No type."

"Pardon?"

"No type, no video, no answer."

"Defiance? This late in the game? And you are so close to the lightening round."

The man in the chair tracked the voice. Although he was barely able to hold his head up, he shifted his eyes to the left. He was certain that was where the knife wielding maniac was standing.

Which was why he was shocked when someone grabbed his right arm. The top of a big, bald head filled his vision. Johnson lashed out, trying to butt heads, but his assailant was just out of his reach.

Strong hands gripped his forearm. They were rough, calloused, bare. These were not the hands which held the knife, but they could have been belonged to whomever had hit him last.

One of the hands remained on his forearm while the other gripped the sodden towel. There was a moment of probing, then the grip tightened around his remaining finger. The hand twisted and pulled. There was a snap, then the feeling of something tearing.

The towel dropped to the floor with a wet plop. It was the last sound the man in the chair heard for quite a while.

LIKE A SWIMMER RISING to the surface, Johnson slowly regained consciousness. Something had changed. The quality of the light was different. How long had he been out this time?

The pain which lanced through his right arm all but drowned out the steady throb of his left. Still, around it all, he felt a different kind of discomfort. He looked down and saw tubing running from a needle in his arm and disappearing somewhere behind his head. A yellowish fluid was being pumped into his vein.

A glance at his right arm showed that it was missing. It could not be missing, it hurt too much to not be there. He shook his head, focused. His right arm was no longer strapped to the arm rest of the chair. A plank of wood was affixed to the chair, creating a second arm rest on that side. This one rose up at a 60 degree angle. His right arm was suspended from it. The hand was completely wrapped in gauze stained pink with his blood. All except for the thumb, which sat naked and alone on the wood.

Despite being raised above the level of his heart, blood continued to leak from the ruined hand. As he watched a fat drop collected at the end of the board and dropped to the ground. From the sound it made, Johnson could tell that it landed in a substantial puddle.

The voice returned.

"Ah, you are awake again. We had to intervene after that last incorrect answer."

The man in the chair could not tell where the voice was coming from. It seemed to be all around him.

"Now then, we are growing short on time and you are running short of fingers. How about we work through these last few questions quickly?"

The voice was not coming from anywhere in the room. It was coming from inside his head. He nodded.

"Good. What was that first video?"

Although his mind screamed for him to remain silent, his lips began moving immediately.

"A little girl, blonde. She was tied face down over a table or a bench or something."

"Did that arouse you?"

"No, yes." He steeled himself for the knife. When it did not come, he continued.

"I was aroused, but not sexually. Something stirred in me. I liked that she was under someone else's control. I wanted to be the person in control."

"Is that why you joined the site?"

"Not really," he hurried on before he could be punished for the non-answer. "It wasn't just the video, it was the contest. I joined the website, then paid the extra fee to enter the contest."

He sighed. The cotton feeling in his head was isolating him from the pain. His wounded limbs felt very far away.

"Every month there was a new video. Every month it was different."

Somehow he thought that the owner of the voice knew all of this. His mind was working furiously. There was something, a revelation, just out of his reach. Meanwhile, he kept talking.

"Some months it was just someone begging, crying, pleading. Other months it was torture. The good months were when there was both."

Pacing, just outside of the reach of the lightbulb.

"Every month there was that little box. 'Enter here for a chance to be the star of next month's video.' I was surprised to find that there was a fee."

"But you paid every month, didn't you?"

"Yes, fifty dollars, every month. I wanted to win. I wanted to be the one in control. I wanted to be the star…"

His words trailed off. His mind finally made the leap.

"Oh."

It was all that he could say. The silence stretched for an eternity marked only by the dripping of his blood.

"You understand now."

Statement, not a question, but it still seemed to require an answer.

"Yes, I understand. I won."

"Yes, yes you did."

"So what happens now?"

"The game is almost over. Only a few more questions. Do you think you can go on?"

The note of concern in the voice startled the man in the chair. He thought about the question for a moment, then nodded.

"Good. Thank you. Now, what, would you say, is your type? What are you attracted to?"

That question again. He mumbled his answer.

"No type, no age, just the scenario."

"What is the scenario?"

"Helpless."

A moment of silence followed. The word seemed to fly around the room, hiding in the dark corners.

"Explain."

"Helpless. At my mercy. Bound, weak, scared, unable to …"

The man in the chair trailed off.

"Like me," he said finally.

"How like you?"

"Not like how I am right now, at this moment. Although, yes, like me right now, all tied up. But also like I am outside here. Caught up in everything, trapped by life."

He looked up and saw the owner of the voice step into the pale circle of light. He was a very plain man. He was short, pale. He had a trim mustache and small eyes. A bit of black hair poked out from beneath the plastic poncho he wore. The poncho was splattered with clotting blood.

His blood.

The blue surgical gloves covered his hands. The right hand held the knife. It looked smaller now, less important.

"Last question, Mr. Johnson."

The man in the chair closed his eyes.

"You have answered a lot of questions tonight. You have divulged a lot about yourself, perhaps things you did not even know until you said them."

Johnson nodded, eyes still closed. He sobbed once, quietly.

"Given all that you have learned, all that you know about yourself now, and considering all that happened tonight, do you want to return to that life? Do you want to continue to be, how did you put it, trapped by life? "

Johnson's eyes remained closed. A tear traced its way down his cheek. As with many of the questions which had come before, the answer to this one was too horrible to contemplate.

The last question is always the hardest to answer.

"No," he said in the strongest voice he could muster. "No, I do not."

There was movement again. This time he could track it not only by sound, but by the play of the light on his eyelids. The steps went from directly in front of him, off to the side, then behind him, light, to dark, to light.

Had he answered all twenty questions? It seemed like more, but then there had been some repetitions, some which had surely not counted. First he had won the website prize, now he had won again.

Winning was a strange thing.

He sighed again, eyes still closed, and let his head fall back against the back of the chair. He raised his chin towards the ceiling, and claimed his prize.

THE KNIFE ENTERED the light one last time, one final arc. It bit deep, moving left to right, along the neck of the man in the chair. It severed both jugular veins and both carotids. It sawed into the trachea. Blood splashed, spurted. Air from the damaged trachea turned the vital fluid into a fine red mist. The owner of the voice stepped back.

The man in the chair thrashed once, twice, then was still.

There was a moment of silence. Then the lights flickered on. Fluorescent tubes cast a harsh glow upon the body in the chair. They revealed the rest of the room, a large concrete box. Positioned outside the area which had been illuminated by the overhead lightbulb were three cameras on tripods. One sat directly in front of the chair, one on either side. Another two cameras were suspended from the ceiling..

A large man with a bald head stepped over to the chair. He wore long gloves which encased his arms to the elbow in black rubber. He began picking up the towels which littered the floor and dumping them in the lap of the body on the chair. He pulled out the IV with one tug, dropped the bag onto the towels. Then he began walking in a slow spiral out from the body. His eyes were cast down on the floor.

The overhead cameras were lowered. A slight man in jeans and flannel collected the small cassette tapes from each of the cameras and placed them in a leather satchel. Then he began breaking down the cameras and tripods.

The man with the voice walked over to him. He had discarded the poncho and gloves. The knife was nowhere to be seen.

"How long before it's ready?" he asked.

"Give me a few hours to run through all of the footage. Another few to cut it together. I should have the rough copies for you tomorrow night, the next morning at the latest. Do you want audio?"

The big man had finished examining the floor. He placed a finger into a tupperware bowel. He looked puzzled. His eyes squinted, then opened wide. He walked over to the chair, picked up the towels and began to shake them open. An index finger fell from one. The big man smiled.

"Give me one copy with, another without," the voice answered.

"OK, then I will need a little more time to distort your voice. All told, we should be ready to upload the new video in a few days."

"Then we can pick another lucky contestant."

RAGNAROK AROUND THE CLOCK

Of all of the places to end up when the end of the world rolled around, Dan Lindstrom ended up in New Oslo. It was a measure of the kind of luck he had been dealing with his entire life. If he had been in his tiny third story walk up he would have simply winked out of existence like the rest of New York City. He could have been in Los Angeles and drowned as the rising oceans reacted to global warming and swamped the city. Instead, he was in New Oslo listening to the other residents and visitors bicker. His life up to that point had been a series of missteps and wrong turns all of which lead him to finding himself in a tiny north woods town when the apocalypse rolled in.

He took another sip of lingonberry flavored tea and stared out of the window. Swede Anne's Coffee Shoppe was half full of 'survivors.' Their voices washed over him, the world's most monotonous wave. The same conversation had been going on for a week.

"I think we can get out on the North Road. There shouldn't be anyone there."

"The North Road doesn't go anywhere but the woods. What are you going to do, live on tree bark and deer crap? No, the thing to do is sneak down Seventh to the Old Mayal Bridge. Then we follow the Serpentine down to Chet's. There should be a couple of canoes or kayaks or something there. We pile in and let the river take us out of town."

Dan closed his eyes. A sigh escaped him. He leaned his head back against the wall, tilting the chair back on two legs. It had been like this for days. All of the dozen or so people hiding in the boarded up building had their own ideas of where they could find safety. Each one felt compelled to not only share it with everyone else, but to try and convince everyone else to go with them.

What they all failed to understand was that there was no safe haven anymore. It was the end of the world. There was no place they could go to escape the apocalypse.

The best they could hope for was a slightly different apocalypse.

"There's nothing downriver but Cooperton." The singsong lilt of the speaker tagged her as a resident. "I figure they are as bad off as we are if not worse. At least we still have power."

"You can live without power," said the first speaker. "At least I can. I've been hunting these woods since I was six."

"Great, fifty odd years and you've never bagged anything bigger than a ground squirrel. I'm telling you the river is the way to go. We don't have to stop at Cooperton. We portage right down Main Street…"

"And go where?" Dan could take no more. His chair crashed back to the floor. All eyes were on the outlander. He rose to his feet before continuing.

"Where would you go? I can guaran-damn-tee that Cooperton is just as bad off as we are here in New Oslo. Tannenbaum is going through the same stuff as we are, but they've got to deal with a crazed Santa as well. Haven't you been watching the news? It's the end of the freaking world."

Stunned silence filled the room. Dan fixed each of the people sitting there with a momentary stare before passing on to the next. There was a lot of blonde hair in this room, many blue eyes.

"Or to be more precise, it's the ends of the freaking world."

He slumped back into his chair and tried to ignore the debate which began anew. He closed his eyes when the conversation turned, inevitably, to the vikings.

Dan had a theory. It had first popped into his head when the story of Saul's Corner hit the news. This was back when there were still news broadcasts, before Los Angeles had been consumed by fires, mudslides, earthquakes, and floods of cinematic proportion. It was before cynical, agnostic New York City simply vanished.

Caleb Baxter was the preacher whose flock was being tormented by Death, War, Pestilence, and Famine. The supernatural beings killed indiscriminately yet never spoke above a whisper. Father Caleb was a grade school dropout who had received his calling late in life. He was almost completely illiterate and had never read the Scriptures. He had, however, listened to all thirty-five cassettes of The Audio Bible. He did not know about homonyms, so perhaps the misunderstanding regarding the Four Horsemen of the Apocalypse could be forgiven.

The second clue had come from the refugees from Tannenbaum, a town a few miles to the west where it was CHRISTMAS EVERY DAY OF THE YEAR. It was a great way to increase tourism, but the people who lived and worked there hated Christmas, reindeer, elves, and especially Santa. They knew that "jolly old elf" was actually a mean old drunk in a bad smelling red suit. When the end of the world came to Tannenbaum, it did so in the form of marauding elves led by an evil Kringle.

Dan's theory consisted of three simple conclusions:

It was the end of the world.

Everyone had a different idea of what this meant.

The Apocalypse was democratic.

Simply put, the dominant belief of any given area dictated how that particular portion of the world would end. Los Angeles went out like a summer blockbuster. Saul's Corner got their ridiculous Hoarse Men. Tannenbaum had psycho Santa.

New Oslo was populated by the descendants of Swedes, Norwegians, and Finns who had moved to Michigan's Upper Peninsula and taken jobs in the mines and the mills. They had brought with them tales of Vikings and the Norse gods.

New Oslo had Valkyries.

SOMEONE BEGAN BANGING on the door. The people holed up in the coffee shop looked at each other for only a moment before their eyes dropped back to their laps. The frosted glass rattled in its frame.

"Someone please." The voice was quiet, pleading. "Open the door. They're almost here."

Dan had to strain to hear the words. The almost whisper was at odds with the loud knocking which had preceded it. He glanced at the furniture comprising the makeshift barricade. He turned towards the door, took one step, then swallowed hard. His throat had suddenly become dry. He sat heavily. The knocking resumed. Dan turned away from the pleas and reached for his tea. It was cold, bitter and tasted like rotted fruit and ashes. He took a long drink to wash down the acid rising in his throat.

The knocking stopped. One by one the patrons glanced back to the door. Dan thought he heard footsteps but would not have been able to swear to it. The knocking resumed a few doors down, the hardware store if Dan remembered Main Street correctly.

There was no mistaking the sound of hoofbeats clacking along the pavement. One moment it was quiet, the next the street was alive with the sound of thunder. Dan did not need to see the scene to know what had happened, what was about to happen. The episode had played out for him once already.

Once was enough.

He moved to the window despite himself.

There were two this time. When he had first witnessed the Valkyries' arrival there had been more, at least a dozen. They had descended from the clouds, their steeds running in the air. They did not break stride as their hooves touched the ground.

The two charging down the street looked much like the ones Dan had seen before. They could have even been two of the ones he had seen before. They all looked similar, long blonde braids streaming behind them. The sunlight gleamed off the brass of their breastplates and their winged helms.

The knocker had noticed the pair as well. The quiet knocking was replaced by a pounding.

"Please!" The voice pitched higher with each word. "For the love of God, please!"

From his vantage point, Dan could not see the panicked man. He had no problem seeing the Valkyries. They stormed by the window, one down the center of the street, one on the sidewalk inches from the building.

The knot of people who had gathered at the window with Dan took a collective step back.

The street bound warrior carried an impossibly long spear balanced easily in one hand. The closer one drew a sword as she rode by. The blade gleamed in the light of the setting sun. If asked, Dan would have said the the metal itself was on fire, not simply reflecting the red-orange light of the dying day.

As the pair rode by, the sword-bearer turned and looked at the coffee shop window. The people inside scattered. Dan held his ground, rooted in place by the Valkyrie's icy stare. Her eyes were the flat blue grey of a northern sea during a winter storm. As their eyes locked, she shimmered. Her edges became less defined. Her body was somehow less solid.

The brass and steel chest plate and chain mail skirt she had been wearing disappeared. Her garb was replaced by a flowing robe of white. Her blonde hair cascaded down her back in a soft wave. The two locked eyes for only a second, but in that time Dan felt a sense of love and compassion that had been missing from his life for years.

Then the screaming started.

The man who had been pounding on the shop door ran out into the street. His shriek had lost all pretense at speech. Dan could see the man. He was short, balding, carrying the sloth of his advanced years in a band which encircled his waist. He moved from the cover of hardware store entrance way to the middle of the street. He charged towards the pair, screaming, running a weaving pattern, his gut bouncing with each footfall.

It was suicide, nothing more. He had decided that he would rather his death be quick than slow. Perhaps he even entertained ideas of taking one of the Valkyrie with him or at least hurting one of them. It was an insane idea. How could a man hope to harm one of the handmaidens of the gods?

The man cut right as if to pass both of them in the street. The spear bearer shifted her weapon. She brought the shaft along the left side of her mount's head. Dan had a brief flash of a jousting exhibition he had seen at a Renaissance Festival years before.

With more agility than Dan would have credited him with, the man cut left again. In a flash the spear bearer was past him, weapon out of position, unable to do much more than turn and watch him go by.

He had a chance.

The scream turned into a cry of triumph as the little man ran between the Valkyrie. Once through he could cut through the alley at the end of the coffee shop or sprint for the tree line. Three more steps and he would be past them.

The swords-woman, the one which had held Dan's gaze for what seemed like a compressed eternity, was too fast for him. Her foot lashed out. It caught the runner in the temple and he crumpled to the street. His cry died in his throat. He raised himself to his hands and feet. He shook his head to clear it. Even from a distance, Dan could see the fine spray of blood which flew off. His scalp bore a deep gash. Blood gushed down the side of his face.

There was another scream, this one from the Valkyrie with the spear. There were no words, just an audible embodiment of rage. Dan clapped his hands to his ears, ducked his head. He was sure the window would explode inward from the force of the goddess' screech.

Her horse reared up, front hooves slicing the air. It pranced like this for a few steps until it was faced back the way it came. Perched high in the saddle, the Valkyrie and her mount appeared as one fearsome giant. She held the spear high above her head. The horse returned to all fours. As it dropped, the arm of the Valkyrie blurred. A bright flash marked the movement of the spear. It flew with all of the force of the horse's movement and the supernatural strength of its rider. If pressed, Dan would swear that he saw the spear spiraling around its midline as it flew true. One moment it was in the Valkyrie's hand. The next it was pinning the man to the ground.

He screamed once more. A crimson gout of blood accompanied the sound. The blood flew from his mouth, a spreading fan of his lost vitality. The spear had pierced his back high between the shoulder blades. It exited the front, below the ribs, and buried itself deep in the blacktop of the street.

The dead man, for this is essentially what he was at this point, still struggled to get his feet beneath him. He managed to get his left foot beneath him. He pushed up, raised himself to a half crouch before the foot slipped and he flopped back, sliding down the length of the spear shaft, hitting the ground hard.

The long column of wood was smeared with his blood and something darker, something which bespoke of death. It marked his movements as futile. He flopped against the street, boneless, twitching muscles connected to a brain which did yet comprehend its end.

The second Valkyrie rode slowly back down the street. She glanced at the coffee shop, but did not meet Dan's eyes. He desperately sought her gaze. She would not look at him. Instead she led her horse, a high stepping prance, to where the dying man lay. She leaned low, so low that she disappeared from view for a moment. There was a flash of flame red metal, a final spray of blood red liquid. She rose up again, slowly, deliberately. When she met Dan's gaze, the compassion that had once lived in her eyes was gone. Only hatred gleamed forth.

Her horse went from a prance, to a trot, from a trot to a gallop. A few paces later it was airborne, galloping across the sky. Her companion rode quickly up the street. She grabbed her spear without slowing. The still bleeding corpse was lifted into the air along with a piece of the tarmac. With a flick of her wrist, she sent corpse and concrete flying. The body hit the street and rolled until it caught against the curb. The horse whinnied as it took to the air. A trail of blood droplets marked its passing.

Dan felt his gorge rise as he looked back to the middle of the street. The man's head still sat there. Its eyes were wide, mouth a gaping hole, still screaming in silent terror.

Dan turned from the window, swallowing hard. He felt the bile burn at the back of his mouth.

He needed more tea.

It was the final piece of the theory. More importantly, it was Dan's way out. He had seen the Valkyrie shimmer. For just a moment she had ceased to be the warrior woman of cartoons and bad made-for-cable movies and had looked like something else.

She had looked like a hand-maiden of Odin, someone charged with bringing the spirits of the fallen to their final reward.

The Valkyrie had become the very embodiment of the characters his Mor-Mor had told him as a child. The change had happened the moment that Dan had made eye contact with her. For just a moment they had connected and she had stopped being what everyone else thought a Valkyrie was and had become what Dan knew them to be.

There was no way to survive the coming apocalypse. He and the others in the coffee shop would not last long. Rather than suffer on earth, why not take his place among the gods? He could be immortal. The means to achieve this was right outside. All he would have to do is convince the others of this.

He looked around the room. Many of the occupants were sitting alone or in pairs. Their eyes were either wide with shock or closed in exhaustion. One table in the back held six people. Dan almost screamed when he realized they were still discussing escape options.

Instead, he stood. Most of the survivors turned towards him. He rapped on the table until he had everyones attention.

"You can stop trying to figure out where to go and how to get there. I have a plan."

Canoe guy's face hardened. He was not going to accept anyone else's ideas. That was fine with Dan. There were bound to be a few casualties. The rest regarded him with looks that ranged from cautious optimism to vague disbelief.

"The Valkyrie," he began.

"The what now?"

Dan was not sure who had asked the question. He closed his eyes and took a deep breath.

"The scary ladies on horseback with the big sharp pointy things are Valkyrie."

He could not keep the derision out of his voice. A few more expressions switched towards disbelief.

"As I am sure most of you know, in Norse mythology the Valkyrie are tasked with finding the souls of brave warriors and taking them up to Valhalla. There they live forever…"

A different voice interrupted him.

"I doubt that the guy who got impaled today would agree with you. He seems more dead than immortal."

"That is because you are not thinking about the Valkyrie as they are. You are mixing them up with all kinds of other characters. They are supposed to be peaceful."

A flurry of questions followed.

"Then how come they have swords?"

"How can a mythological character kill anyone? Those things out there are real."

"Yeah, how come they are killing everyone?"

Dan held up his hand.

"Because you expect them to do exactly that. If you all believe that they are…"

"Are you saying that this is our fault?"

Before he could answer, someone at the back table spoke up. It was the flannel clad proponent of living in the woods.

"Don't look at it as fault. Look at it as opportunity."

Dan was amazed. He had expected a lot more explaining before anyone was convinced. He had expected those seated at the back table to be among the last to accept the idea, if at all.

"What this guy, sorry son, never did get your name."

"Dan, Dan Lindstrom, my mother…"

Flannel Man waved off the explanation.

"What he is saying is that if we stop thinking of them being out to get us, they will stop being out to get us."

"That makes less than no sense at all," said the guy with the canoe plan.

"Look at Tannenbaum," Dan said. "They expected bad stuff from Santa Claus and they got just what they imagined. If you think about it, it does make sense."

"Are you saying we don't have any sense?" Canoe Guy leapt to his feet.

"Shut up and sit down, Elim. What he is saying is that if we stop thinking about these, whatchcallit, Valkyries as killers we have a chance."

"Exactly."

"What we all have to do is think about them as weak and defenseless. Once we have that image fixed in our minds, we can rush them."

"Rush them?" Dan's brow furrowed. "Why would we rush them?"

"Right, why not just escape?"

Dan turned towards the direction of the new speaker. Flannel Man would have none of it.

"Because once we stop thinking about them as weak they will come after us again."

"No, that's not it at all." No one seemed to hear Dan's protest.

"Why don't we just stop thinking about them all together? Wouldn't they just disappear?"

"You can't not think about something. Try not thinking about a purple cow. No, we imagine them weak, then we make a break for it. If we scatter we will increase the chances that some of us will get free."

Dan silently pushed his chair in. He threaded his way between the tables and back into the kitchen. He closed the door behind him. A sob escaped him.

It was hopeless. He could not get them to agree on anything. Half of them did not even know their own heritage. They might be able to think the Valkyrie into the proper shape, but it would not last. Without a fixed image of what the Valkyrie were supposed to be they would undoubtedly go back to thinking of them as executioners. His belief alone would not be enough to save him. Anyone out there at that time would be run through.

The arguing became loud enough for Dan to hear through the kitchen door. There was a shout, almost a bark of surprise. There was a loud crash.

If only there were a way to get them to all stop thinking at once.

Dan looked around the kitchen. For a coffee shop, it had a

surprisingly large amount of cutlery. He started to smile as he added another conclusion to his theory.

DAN STEPPED out into the street. He dragged a hand across his brow, wiping away residual blood. His hand was still wrapped around a six inch carving knife. Hoofbeats echoed from the next block over. Dan stood in the center of Main Street. The hoof falls stopped abruptly. Dan dropped the knife and stepped away from it.

There were two Valkyrie, one at either end of the town. Dan was not sure, but he thought that they might be the two from the previous day. He focused on the closer of the two. He concentrated on everything he knew about the handmaidens of Odin.

As the woman bore down on him she began to change. Once again the breast plate and spear disappeared to be replaced by the long flowing white robes. She smiled a beatific smile. She drew still nearer. Her horse slowed to a walk. The hand which had once held a spear was now outstretched. She leaned over the thickly muscled neck of her steed, reaching for him.

As she did, Dan could see that it was indeed the Valkyrie from the day before. Her blue eyes sparkled the way they had when she had first shimmered and then changed. Gone was the hard, angry look she had had when she drew her sword.

"I'm ready," Dan called.

Her visage seemed to flicker, just for a moment. Dan tried desperately to cling to the image of the angelic woman on horseback. He wanted only to see the kind being that was going to take him away from all of the fear and insanity that marked everyday life. He wanted to see the woman who would bear him up to the Viking heaven and not the warrior with the sword.

"No, no. I understand what you are. I am ready to be taken up to Valhalla."

"You are bloodied."

The voice of the Valkyrie sounded like winter wind.

"I...I did what needed to be done."

The Valkyrie's eyes darkened once more. Her soft features flowed. The gentle roundness disappeared. Her cheeks stood out as sharp lines on the angled plane of her face. Her eyes narrowed.

"You are bloodied, but not from battle. You are bloodied, but you are not Einherjar."

"No, no wait."

Dan started to move backwards, one step, then two, then half a dozen. He glanced down at the knife. She drew her flaming sword with a slow, deliberate motion. As he turned to run, Dan saw her eye flicker once more showing something, pity or glee, he was not sure which.

Then he felt the cold bite of the steel.

THE SANDWICH YEARS

JANEY NEEDED BRACES, Bill new shoes. Tuition, mortgage, and life insurance bills awaited payment.

Jim sat listening to the whir of his father's respirator.

THE PERFECT ANNIVERSARY PRESENT

THE DOG WHINED and pawed at the soft earth.

"Come," she called, patting her leg.

"No, Officer. I haven't seen him for days."

DID YOU GET THAT?

Ryan Grant was a putz.

He knew that it was uncharitable to think it, but Steve Wilson could not get around the fact that his latest assignment was to haul around nearly one hundred pounds of video equipment and try desperately to make a complete putz look good.

"But I don't want to wear the hard hat."

The voice which emanated from the back of the van sound nothing like the smooth, almost syrupy unaccented tones of the on air personality. It more closely resembled the whine of a young child being told that he had to go to bed while all of the grown-ups got to stay up later. It also had a healthy dose of twang which marked its owner as a son of the deep South.

Wilson wondered what would happen if Grant appeared before the camera and reported the news in his natural voice. He also wondered how much Grant had paid a vocal coach to rid him of his aural roots in favor of the non-accent favored by the national network types.

Wilson checked over his gear once more. For now, the weather was holding, but he knew that would change soon. His set-up should be able to handle anything that Mother Nature would throw at them, but it never hurt to be sure.

From the van Wilson heard a producer's voice over the speakerphone desperately trying to talk Grant into wearing the hard hat.

"Yes, but if you are wearing the safety gear then no one will see your hair so no one will know that it has been 'mussed.'"

"Exactly my point, no one will see my hair. You don't rise up to the national level without good hair."

Wilson sighed and pulled a battered laptop out of his gear bag. He searched through some files he had recently downloaded from the network's library. He found the one he wanted easily. It was a short clip, maybe five minutes long. It showed an old Japanese man chained to a tree while a number of people talked to him. In the distance, you could see the sky darkening.

Wilson found the portion of the clip he wanted. It showed a young child, the old man's grandson, pleading with him while the Pacific boiled. Wilson saved the clip and sent it to the producers. A few moments later, the computer pinged.

He checked his e-mail. There was one new message in his inbox.

PERFECT. GREAT COUNTER-POINT. CAN YOU GET GRANT TO WEAR THE HARD HAT?

Wilson turned off the computer without replying. He slid the laptop back in the bag and walked back to the van.

Ryan Grant, tanned, perfectly coiffed, turned his cosmetically enhanced blue eyes to look at Wilson.

"Can you believe it? They want me to wear a hard hat?"

When Wilson did not reply with the appropriate outrage, Grant continued.

"On camera!"

Wilson looked at the offending head-ware. It was bright yellow. The only distinguishing mark it bore was the network's logo. There were no scratches or scuffs anywhere on it. It appeared brand new.

"It's not that bad," Wilson said. "It reminds me of the imbedded journalists in Iraq."

"Not that bad?" Grant replied, then cut off in mid rant. "Imbedded journalists?"

"Yeah, you know, helmets and flak jackets, reporting from the front lines."

"Like Katie Couric?"

Wilson nodded. He had actually been thinking of Bob Woodruff and Brian Wilson, but if it would take comparison to Katie Couric to get Grant to go along with the program, then so be it.

"All right, hand me that thing."

He scooped up the hard hat and plopped it on his head, wincing as it touched his hair. Wilson thought he heard Grant's hair crunch as the helmet came into contact with layers of styling product. Which gave him an idea.

"Besides, you would not want to look too good while you are out there. You want to give the impression that you are facing grave danger to bring the people this story. No one will believe you if you look as if you just stepped out of a salon. But this…"

He pointed at the hard hat. Grant smiled, then turned to the make-up mirror attached to the interior wall of the van. He began the laborious process of checking himself from each angle, making sure he looked just right.

Wilson stepped out of the van. He tugged on the brim of his baseball cap, the only head protection he would be wearing.

He had been accurate when he had said 'the impression' of danger. He knew full well that Grant would never actually put himself in jeopardy. In fact, the only reason he had been willing to report from the field was that it was an opportunity for national exposure with minimal risk.

Grant was essentially a coward.

Wilson, on the other hand, had joined the network after leaving military service. After his discharge, he had been left with a deep need to show the world the kind of horrors which he himself had lived through. Some people thought the he volunteered for dangerous assignments because he was an adrenaline junkie. This was not so, but he did have a reputation for taking risks to get a shot.

At least until he had been teamed up with Ryan Grant. Since then he had spent a lot of time following Grant from one cushy assignment to another. The boredom was slowly making him insane. He had decided that the only way to get back to the action of reporting real news was to rid himself of Grant. The only way that was going to happen was if Grant got promoted.

Which meant he was going to have to be noticed by one of the big wigs up at the main office.

Hence the trip out to one of the oddest protests anyone had seen in quite a while. It consisted of a single protestor who was chained to a tree. Wilson looked over at him. He waved. Wilson waved back. He checked the ambient light with a hand held light meter. Then he gathered his camera and equipment and headed over to the tree. He was hailed before he could reach it.

"How are you doing over there?" The man had the tanned, rawhide look of a lifelong beachcomber, but his words spoke of northern origin. His greeting sounded like "Howayah doin oertha" and it took Wilson a moment to decipher it.

"No problems here. The question is how are you doing?"

"Oh, I'm fine." I'm fahn. "I've weathered worse than this. If an eighty year old Japanese man can do it, so can I. Besides, it's for a good cause."

"Yes it is," Wilson said. "Ryan Grant will be along in a moment to interview you and you can get your message out to everyone."

"Grant? That putz? I was hoping for one of the pretty news anchors. Well, I suppose Grant is pretty in his own way."

Wilson looked down and pretended to be checking the setting on the camera. He waited until he was sure that the laughter which had threatened to burst out was under control before looking up. When he did, he saw Grant striding down the hill. He wore a blue nylon jacket with the station's logo on the breast. Beneath it one could catch a glimpse of his snow white shirt and red and blue striped tie.

He was not wearing the hard hat. His hair was completely still, despite the growing wind coming in from the ocean.

"Oh, here comes the putz now."

Perhaps the wind covered the old man's words. If not, Grant did an excellent job of pretending that he had not heard.

"Hello," he said when he reached them. "I am Ryan Grant, Channel Six news. You probably recognize me."

DID YOU GET THAT?

Both Wilson and the old man muttered "putz" under their breaths.

"We still have a few minutes before we go live with the national feed," Wilson explained. "I need to check my audio levels. Why don't you give us a little background so we can make sure we have everything correct?"

There was no need to check anything. This was Wilson's way of covering Grant's ass. If the interviewees went over things before they were on camera, the chances of them freezing up later went way down. It also decreased the chances of Wilson screwing up something little. The name of the person being interviewed, for example, or perhaps the reason that they were there.

"Right, great idea."

Wilson slipped on a pair of headphones, then lifted the video camera to his shoulder. He sighted on the old man's face. Framed in the view finder, he looked like Popeye's father.

"My name is Herbert Lindstrom. I have lived here in Oceanside for the last twenty years."

He raised his eyebrows at the newsmen. Wilson gave him a thumbs up.

"I was here five years ago when we had the last Kaiju attack. I evacuated with everyone else, then got to watch the fiasco on television, just like everyone else."

"Wow, that's great," Wilson said in a condescending tone. "Did you get that?

There was a buzz of static in the headphones which stopped Wilson from replying. He held up a hand.

"National feed coming to you in thirty," said a tinny voice.

"We're live in thirty," Wilson repeated.

Lindstrom straightened a bit against the tree. Grant slipped an earpiece into one ear, then smoothed his hands over his hair before placing the offending hard hat over it.

"Sibilant, sibilant," Grant said quietly. "Moses supposes his toeses are roses, yet Moses supposes erroneously."

"Live in ten," said the voice.

"For Moses he knowses his toeses aren't roses."

"Five."

123

Wilson held up one hand, five fingers spread.

"Four,"

He ticked off one finger.

"As Moses supposes his toeses to be."

"Three."

The voice was replaced by the network theme music. There was a momentary pause, then another voice filled Wilson's headphone. It belonged to the man sitting in the anchor chair which Grant coveted.

"As the southeast is preparing for another onslaught, we are reminded of Tanji Oshi, a man who, a few years ago, refused to evacuate Chiba City in the face of its eminent destruction."

Wilson knew that the footage he had found in the archives would be playing over the anchor's shoulder.

"This scene is being replayed here in the U. S. in what is being described as both an homage and a protest. We go live to Oceanside."

Wilson pointed at Grant. The light on top of the camera winked on. Grant looked into the lens and gave the viewers his serious look.

"Thank you Brad. Ryan Grant, here. We are not far from the Oceanside Boardwalk, an area that is usually filled with happy people relaxing and enjoying a day by the sea. The eminent attack has left the boardwalk all but empty. Empty save for one man,"

There was a long pause.

Oh crap, he forgot the name.

"That man," Grant said, turning to face the tree, "is Herbert Lindstrom."

Wilson sighed with relief.

"Mr. Lindstrom, can you tell us what you are doing and why you are doing it?"

Wilson panned over, excluding Grant from the shot. He started with a full length view which showed Lindstrom in his yellow Hawaiian shirt, khaki board shorts, and flip flops. The length of chain wrapped around his waist gleamed dully. As he began to speak, Wilson zoomed in until he had a tight shot of the man's lined face and scraggly gray whiskers.

"I have lived in Oceanview for over twenty years." Wilson's voice was strong. "I have seen all kinds of natural disasters, everything from tropical storms and tsunami to mutant bugs and giant lizards. In all those years I never saw anything like the debacle that happened five years ago.

"No one was prepared, not the local or state governments, not the Feds or any of their agencies. They evacuated thousands of people, left thousands more behind. I am so tired of people complaining about the ones who stay behind. They don't seem to realize that some people can't leave. They have families, animals, lives that they can't take with them. Sure, there are some very wealthy people living down here on the beach. Most of them just leave for their summer places further north. Most of the people down here are poor. I am talking about no car, walk everywhere poor. People like that can't just leave at a moment's notice."

Wilson felt, more than saw Grant hovering at the edge of the shot. He ignored the reporter and kept the focus on Lindstrom.

"I was one of the ones that left. I came back to ruins. And it wasn't looters, like everyone always says, it was just the sheer destructive force of the creature. I was lucky. I was in the army, I know how to live in a tent for months at a time. Most other people don't. There were families all crowded into those 'temporary shelters.' Nothing more than a tractor trailer. You can't raise kids in a tractor trailer!"

"Certainly the government has helped with the rebuilding effort." Grant's voice, off camera.

"Pah! Do you know who helped us rebuild? The same people that helped us get out. Good Samaritans, normal people from all over. Right after that thing was subdued they started coming. Texans in pick-up trucks, flat boats from Louisiana, doctors and nurses on their vacations. The only reason that Oceanside is a living city again is because everyone pitched in and helped their neighbors. If one man has a hammer and his neighbor didn't, he loaned him the thing. If someone had some extra food and someone else was hungry, they shared."

"So Oceanside came together in a spirit of sharing to rebuild."

Against his wishes, Wilson pulled back to fit both men in the shot.

"And now all that you have rebuilt is being threatened again."

"Exactly! And there is no need for it to be."

"So you are saying that the government should be doing more to help the people of Oceanside and the surrounding area?"

"Yes, but it is how they help that I have a problem with."

"Assistance to those in need after a Kaiju disaster has been a topic of discussion at the conventions for both parties."

"Oh yes, the parties!" Lindstrom rolled his eyes. "Isn't it great how they both scaled back their conventions in the face of this attack. Of course, none of them are actually down here, none of the money which is not being spent up there is being sent here. And isn't it a coincidence that the first real attack of the season happens when the party in power is starting their national convention?"

"Surely you don't think that anyone in the government has the ability to prevent monster attacks?"

"I am not saying that they do." Lindstrom was suddenly cagey. His eyes darted around suspiciously. Wilson opened his mouth to ask another question, but was cut off by the man chained to the tree.

"I will say that I find it suspicious that there are no Kaiju attacks on any northern cities. When was the last time a giant fire spewing lizard attacked the east coast? When was the last time that a giant ape ran rampant through Manhattan?"

Fortunately for Grant, the camera was focused solely on Lindstrom. The reporter stood there for a long moment, mouth open, eyes wide. Before Grant could recover, the earth began to shake. A horrible sound rent the air, part squeal, part roar. Wilson paned right. Further out, the ocean was churning. Fog rolled ashore, obscuring their view.

"It would appear that the attack is about to begin in earnest," Grant said. He looked over at Wilson, noticed he was not on camera and mouthed "did you get that?"

Before he could ask Lindstrom the obligatory "How do you feel?" the voice in his ear buzzed.

"Excuse me, Grant, we are going to have to interrupt your interview. Amateur footage of the landing has appeared on-line."

"What? Wait!" Grant said to dead air. Wilson shook his head. He snapped off the camera.

"That's it, Ryan. They cut us off."

"What? They broke the live feed?"

In the headphones, the national anchor was launching into an explanation.

"The footage you are about to see was filmed by internet journalists known as video bloggers or vloggers. It contains images which may be inappropriate for younger viewers."

Wilson wished he was back in the news van so he could watch the video on the uplink. Even more, he wished he was down with the vloggers, not up a hill, tied to a plastic newsman, especially one who was in the middle of an age-inappropriate hissy fit.

"I can't believe they cut away from us! For some crappy amateur footage? I did not even get to sign off."

Wilson had no response. He shrugged.

"Will they be coming back to us? Should we stay here?"

"I don't know for sure, but it does not sound like it." He turned to Lindstrom. "Thank you for your time. I am sorry we were not able to spend more time talking with you."

This was, of course, something that the reporter should have taken care of.

"Oh, thank you for coming down here and letting me get my message out. Feel free to come back down and interview me again, if I am still here that is."

He smiled wryly and looked out at the ocean. The fog and mist had gotten much denser. Somewhere in the middle of it was a dark shape. It was vaguely humanoid, definitely bipedal. It was difficult to gauge heights at that distance, but it appeared to be at least four stories tall.

"This was my big chance. This was my ticket out of rubesville."

Grant's tirade was made ironically amusing by the return of his thick accent. He paced in a tight circle, muttering under his breath. When his orbit took him near Wilson, the cameraman could make out a few words.

"Amateur footage, my show. Ought to be my footage."

Wilson was in the process of wrapping up the microphone cables when Grant came to a sudden stop. He looked up, a mad glare bright in his eyes.

"It will be my footage. My footage, and my ticket out of here."

Wilson cocked an eyebrow at him.

"Come on," Grant said. "If they want footage of the thing coming ashore, then we will give them footage of the thing coming ashore."

He turned and began to jog down towards the beach.

"Footage and a qualified reporter to explain what the people are seeing."

WILSON RAN AFTER GRANT. The reporter's actions had left him so astonished that long minutes passed before he thought to follow him. Grant was halfway down the hill which separated the area where Lindstrom was chained from the beach and the boardwalk. Wilson hefted the camera and took off after the newsman.

He still had his headphones on. He could hear the national producer asking where they were. They had intended to go back to Grant after all. When they realized that there was no image all hell broke loose. The national anchor covered for a moment, then segued easily into a discussion of FEMAs response to the previous Kaiju attack.

His voice was replaced by the voice of the former director of FEMA. Wilson could picture the footage in his mind. Everyone had seen it. The director had fallen on his sword, publicly accepting the blame for the incredible damage and loss of life. His resignation, however, was only the very beginning of the shake-up which would reach to the very pinnacle of politics.

"We at the national level failed our constituents. Our predictions regarding where the beast would make landfall were off by hundreds of miles. Our early reports stated that the giant beetle would do little harm beyond some simple structural damage. We greatly underestimated its strength, we knew nothing of its fire-breathing capability, and our response was uncoordinated and woefully unprepared."

"Start shooting! Start shooting!"

Grant had reached the edge of the boardwalk and had leapt off

DID YOU GET THAT?

into the sand. Somewhere along the way he had lost his yellow hard hat. His hair was actually unkempt. The winds down at the ocean level were fierce. The rolling fog was everywhere.

Wilson shouldered the camera and began shooting. He did his best to keep the image in the viewfinder steady. He centered the camera on Grant and continued running towards him.

The minute he began broadcasting, the voices in the headphones started again.

"We have something."

"Those vloggers?"

"No the local feed."

There was a moment of silence, then a voice said "Put it on."

Grant must have heard this all in his earpiece. He began speaking in his smooth, professional tones.

"Ryan Grant here at Oceanside, ground zero for this latest attack."

Wilson winced.

"As of yet, we have had no clear view of the monster. You may have seen blurry, unprofessional images. We here at channel six are risking all to bring you the latest in this breaking story."

Another horrible roar exploded from the water's edge. Wilson could feel the pressure of the sound waves hit his chest. He panned over to the water. As he did, he heard Grant, sounding suddenly less than professional.

"Holy crap, did you get that?"

Wilson ignored him, trying to get a clear image through the fog. Something huge was moving towards the beach. The water churned, huge waves crashing against the shore. Wilson could feel the spray from where he stood, a good distance away from Grant, who was moving closer to the water.

Water sloshed over Grant's legs as he regained his composure and turned back to the camera.

"We are here, in the path of the creature. As of yet there has been no evidence of government response at any level, federal, state, or local."

Wilson was impressed. Grant was not only keeping his composure, he was tying the new footage into the interview he had just completed.

That increased the chances that the interview, or at least portions of it, would be replayed when this footage was re-aired. That meant more exposure for Grant.

"If you look behind me you can see the…"

Grant trailed off as he looked over his shoulder. Emerging from the fog, shredding it to thin wisps, was something that looked like a cross between an iguana and a chicken, but on a giant scale. It's beak was orange and curved downward to a wicked point. It opened its mouth to roar. The maw was large enough for a small car to dive into. Its eyes smoldered a hellish red.

The body was covered with yellowish green scales. Bat-like wings extended out from the shoulders, ending in sharp talons. Tiny forearms clutched at the air. The muscular legs took one step, two, forcing a mass of water before it.

"Are you getting this?" Grant asked. Then the wave hit him and knocked him from his feet. He struggled to get up, but the back-flow of water dragged him back towards the sea. He screamed once as he scrambled for footing.

Then a giant, taloned foot slammed down, crushing the reporter. The water churned red as the beast let out another terrible scream.

As Wilson ran back up the hill to safety, three thoughts raced through his mind, one after the other. The first was that he had indeed gotten all of the footage. If the uplink was still in place, Ryan Grant's demise had just been broadcast live into millions of homes. Grant had finally gotten the fame he has always wanted.

Wilson hoped that no children had been watching.

The second thought, even worse than the first, was that he was finally free of Grant. He would never have to follow the schmuck around again. If he survived, of course.

Hard on the heels of this was the worst thought yet.

In the end, the hard hat just wouldn't have helped Grant.

CREAK

Eternal life.

Who would not undergo hardship, torture, pain for such a prize?

Who could turn their back on its promise, to stand outside of time, undying and everlasting?

Some, perhaps, upon learning the cost would balk, but not I. Not even the price of the transformation which was almost too horrible to imagine would keep me from trying.

Not even the continuing price would stop me.

The transformation was ungodly and I am now hardly recognizable as the Munchkin I once was. I have taken what was freely given to that fool Chopper. I seized it and have paid for it again and again in blood, blood by the gallons.

All things which live need blood and blood is the price one pays to live.

Creak.

Trapped here, unable to move more than a little in any direction, I can't help but think about the day I decided that I was going to live forever.

There are certain events which define a generation. Everyone remembers where they were when they first heart that the wizard was no more than smoke, mirrors, and an echoey amplified voice. I can't tell you how many people have claimed to have been there when the girl from Kansas arrived with her witch killing flying house. If you believe them all, the entire population of Munchkinland must have been gathered at that spot.

The moment I got The Idea was one of those moments for me. I remember with perfect clarity when the germ of the idea wormed its way into my brain.

It happened the day after I had been diagnosed with the Wasting Disease.

Creak.

Knowing when and how you are going to die is a horrible thing. The worst part of any day was that moment when I was forced to acknowledge my doom. I would awaken refreshed, at peace, still groggy with the shreds of the night's dreams still clinging to my eyes. Then I would remember. The horrible inevitability of it would crash down on my like a leaden weight. Knowing that I had, at best, a year to live would force me back down into the bed. Knowing that for a portion of that year I would be unable to rise from my bed, would have to rely on others to feed me, bathe me, that I would be incapable of caring for myself in anyway would force me back out of the bed.

What horrible thoughts. There are so many other memories on which I can focus: my struggle to stay alive and all that it cost me. The screams and the blood.

Of course, the memories of the blood.

Creak.

I do not remember the days immediately after I was diagnosed, not really. I remember walking around in a fog. I remember working the bellows that fed the furnace. As I stoked the fires I wondered how much longer I would be able to perform my duties. How would I be able to pump in the air to keep the flames high when my muscled arms withered down to skin wrapped sticks? How could I pour the molten lead with hands reduced to twisted, gnarled hooks?

My own worries and the sound of hammers still echoed in my head even after I left the kiln and walked to the Hall of Assembly with the others. They all but pushed the Crier's words from my mind. He was reading the Scarecrow's latest observations on the decline of Oz. Honestly, one would think that the ecological fear mongering had been written by the straw man's feline companion.

From the glazed eyes in the room, I was not the only on who had stopped listening. It was hard to follow the excessively scholarly terminology which polluted all of the Scarecrow's promulgations. The Crier stopped to sip from the cup on the edge of the podium. A collective shiver went through the assembled Munchkins as we all came back to ourselves from wherever our minds had roamed. We leaned forward, hoping the content of the next scroll would be worth the time which we could have spent with our loved ones, spent resting, or relaxing before another grueling day.

"The next announcement," the Crier said in a voice which was high and thin but yet somehow reached the back corners of the Hall of Assembly, "comes from the Emperor of the Winkies, The Tin Woodsman."

He unfastened the clasps which held the leather tube closed. He unrolled a scroll twice again as high as he stood. A groan went through the crowd. Murmurs sprung up here and there as Munchkins wondered aloud how much longer the readings would take.

"People of Winkie Country and residents of the Quadling Country. Gillikins and People of the Munchkin Country, Loyal Servants: I bring you greetings from the Emerald City."

My blood echoed in my ears, drowning out the words the Crier read. Loyal Subjects was galling enough, but to list the People of Munchkinland *last*! After the hammerheads, after the flying monkeys, then he lowered himself to speak to us? My face flushed hot as if I had been standing next to the kiln. How dare he address us so? What made him so special, what lifted him above our lowly station; the trip he took with The Outlander with the Ruby Slippers, his metal skin and ridiculous funnel cap? He was no more than a Munchkin himself, just one who had traded his normal sized body for a giant one made of tin.

I stalked from the Hall of Assembly, unable to stand for any more of the pompous declarations.

A few heads turned to follow me, a few voices whispered.

Fortunately I was far enough in back of the hall that few took notice of my leaving.

The night air was cool on my face. My rage left me. Pity rushed in to fill the void it left behind. It wasn't fair. Few remembered the name Nick Chopper, but all of us metallurgists knew the tale. It was one of our proudest moments. The story of the creation of that metal body, crafted one limb at a time and grafted on to a living Munchkin was one of the reasons I first turned to the craft. I had spent year as an apprentice, tending the fires. Now I would never become a master, never craft my own fine items for sale throughout Munchkinland. The Wasting Disease would take me before year's end.

I had worked hard my whole life and would never see the fruits of my studies. Chopper, falls in love with the Wicked Witch's handmaiden, gets cursed, and now lords over all of Oz. My body would slowly decompose while I still breathed. He cuts off his own limbs and gets them replaced by tin and steel. I would die but that pretentious lumberjack would live forever.

It simply wasn't fair.

I had made it half way back to my tiny house when the though hit me with such force that I was stopped in my tracks. It wasn't fair. I shouldn't have to die young.

If I could repeat what had been done to Nick Chopper I wouldn't have to. Why should he get to live forever in a tin skinned body?

Creak.

If few people remembered the Woodsman's original name, no one remembered the name of the man who created the Woodsman's tin skinned body. At least, no one was willing to speak his name. I did my best to steer conversations towards the creation of the Tin Man. Every conversation ended the same. There would be a little speculation regarding the methods used to fabricate the various body parts. When the conversation turned to the process of melding metal to flesh, all eyes would turn down. Voices would die down to a murmur. There would be a long silence, a silence finally broken by the same word every time.

"Tik Tok."

"Tik Tok, now that's a feat of engineering right there."

CREAK

"Sure, creation of a metal body to replace a real one is impressive, but if you really want to talk about something amazing there's Tik Tok."

Tik Tok, that automaton, that abomination. It was nothing more than a series of gears and springs. Sure, the clockwork movements provided not only movement, but also thought, reason, and emotion.

Yes, it was a brilliant invention.

It would not keep me alive.

Creak.

The knife was pressed against his neck. A thin trickle of blood ran from where the knifepoint dented his wizened flesh.

"You will tell me!" I hollered. The tiny man's eyes widened. In fear? I hoped so. I could only hope that none of my own fear, my desperation, was evident in my voice. I concentrated all of my will on keeping the blade of the small knife steady. It had taken months, but I had finally tracked the old Munchkin to this tiny shack in the middle of the forest.

I lowered my voice. My eyes narrowed to slits. I drew in one quavering breath, then continued.

"I know who you are Ku-Klip. I know what you have done before. I know what you are capable of doing still."

"I don't know what you are talking about," the old man said. "My name is…"

He made a strangled sound as I cut him off by pushing the knife further into his throat. The rivulet became a freshet. His scarred right hand rose as if he meant to staunch the flow of blood before remembering the blade which rested there. His hand hovered at shoulder height.

"Your name is Ku-Klip. You are, were, a tinsmith. Decades ago, Nick Chopper came to you each time his axe lopped off another of his limbs."

Ku-Klip started to shake his head. The movement caused his neck to move beneath the knife blade. He coughed as a new cut appeared. I watched, fascinated as the thin line filled with blood which welled for a moment, then began to trickle.

"You did the same for a military man named Fyter who had the misfortune to fall in love with the same woman Chopper had."

"What do you want?" Ku-Klip had pulled his head back as far as he could. I had backed him into the wall. He turned his head to the side. His cheek pressed into the shelves there.

"I want you to do the same thing for me. I want you to fashion a body to replace this one. I want you to make me into a tin man like you did for Fyter, like you did for Chopper."

"There is only one Nick Chopper and I am he."

The voice boomed out from somewhere above us. My head snapped up to see who had spoken. That moment of inattention almost cost me all.

Ku-Klip was fast for an old Munchkin.

He was much faster than I had given him credit for.

I felt the explosion of pain before I knew what was happening. My vision narrowed to a dim tunnel. I shook my head to clear it, a mistake. The world swam, my head spun. I was only dimly aware of something crashing into my back.

It was the floor.

I crabbed backwards. My empty hands sought anything I could use for a weapon. I had lost the knife. My vision cleared for a moment. I looked around for Ku-Klip but did not see him. Random objects fluttered in and out of view: a chair, the rug beneath my hands, the bookshelf cluttered with pots, bowls, a head which glared at me.

I squeezed my eyes shut. When I opened them I connected again with the glare of a severed head sitting on the bookshelf. It seemed to stare at me.

Then it blinked.

I started to scream. My vision narrowed again until I could see nothing but that head. I didn't see Ku-Klip approaching, didn't see him swing the heavy iron fireplace poker.

I was still screaming when the darkness swept over me.

When my consciousness returned, I found myself trussed to a chair. Ku-Klip was seated across from me. A small, round table separated us. He was idly twirling a knife in one hand.

My knife.

I craned around in the chair, trying to see the rest of the room. We were in a different part of the house. I had no idea how the old Munchkin had been able to drag me out of the front room. Granted, I had lost weight as the disease began to take its toll on me, but I should have been far to heavy for one small man.

Perhaps he had help.

"What are you looking for? Trying to find someone to help you? Looking for a way to escape, perhaps?"

He dabbed at his throat with a bit of rag. The gray cloth was already stiff with dried blood. He smeared the tiny bit of red which still clung to his Adam's apple. Ku-Klip looked at the cloth. His lip rolled up in a sneer.

He leaned forward, halving the distance between us. His breath was fetid. His teeth were twisted and yellowed. I had not noticed that when I had been in charge of the situation, but now that our roles were reversed.

Ku-Klip raised his hand high above his head then slammed the knife into the table. It quivered between us. I saw that the blade was still stained with his blood.

"Now, tell me what you think it is that you know."

I started to lie, but what was the point? I was there to get his help, after all.

"I know that you are Ku-Klip, the tinsmith who made the bodies for the Tin Woodsman and Fyter. I know that you are skilled not only in the ways of metallurgy, but also in the mysticism which is necessary to keep me alive."

He seemed about to protest again, but my last words stopped him. He looked at me for a moment. His eyes gleamed in the candlelight. Finally he lowered himself slowly into the chair across from me.

"What else?"

I shook my head.

"How do I know you were not sent by Princess Ozma, or by the Tin Man himself?"

I stared at him. If I hadn't been bound so tightly to the chair, I would have shrugged my shoulders.

"I do know what you are talking about. I'm just a smith's apprentice."

"So you are telling me that you really don't know? You just happened upon me and thought you would, what?"

"I don't know what you are talking about."

"You say that you know who I am, what I have done."

"Yes, you made tin bodies..."

Ku-Klip cut me off with a wave of his hand.

"Yes, and you of course know why."

"Because..." what was he looking for? "Because they had been cursed by the Wicked Witch. Because she didn't want to lose her servant to marriage."

"And now the Witch is dead and Nimmie Amee is married. So why would you need a tin body?"

"Because like those men, I am dying. I...I have the Wasting Disease. Soon I will be too weak to stand without help."

The old wizard's eyes widened.

"So you want me to craft a body for you so you will not die? You were not sent by...you are here for selfish reasons."

I felt my face flush hot. Ku-Klip continued before I could reply.

"The most understandable and at the same time the most selfish reason. You want to live, perhaps forever. You want to thwart the very nature of the universe. And you want my help doing it."

My head sagged. The ropes were all that kept me from slumping down to the table. The anger and fear had left me. I felt drained. My arms, still lashed to the arms of the chair, began to shake.

I felt a rough hand against my cheek. A row of callouses divided the fingers from the palm. The fingers themselves were crisscrossed with old scars, some from cuts and some from burns. I had similar scars on mine, but mine were mostly smooth, round areas caused by flaming embers. Ku-Klip's were mostly thin lines caused by encounters with sharp pieces of tin.

A gentle but firm pressure lifted my head until I was gazing into Ku-Klip's eyes. He stared at me for a moment. The corner of his mouth twitched.

"If I did this thing for you, what would my reward be?"

"Your reward?"

"You don't think I would do this thing for free, do you?"

"I..."

Ku-Klip's eyes widened. The twitch at the corner of his mouth became a full fledged smile.

"You did! You thought you could simply come here and ask me to do this thing. Or did you think you could threaten me, scare me into doing what you wished?"

"I assumed..."

"You assumed that I was some kindly old man who fashioned living bodies for those who needed them? Perhaps I am a hopeless romantic who rebuilt Chopper and Fyter out of the goodness of my heart."

"Why did help those two, then?"

Before he could answer my question another voice rang out in the small room.

"I am Nick Chopper."

I twisted my head again and wished I had not. I closed my eyes for a moment. When the room stopped spinning, I opened them again. It was still there. Sitting on the top shelf of the cabinet next to two jars was a head. The skin was a waxy and the eyes were dull and lifeless. Beyond that it looked perfectly real.

Especially when it opened its mouth and spoke.

"I say again, I am Nick Chopper and that tin imbecile is an obvious impostor."

A scream began to well in my throat. Ku-Klip stepped over to the cupboard and took down the jars which bookended the head. Without their support it rolled onto its cheek.

"See here," it said.

"Quiet," the tinsmith turned its back on the head. He held out the two jars for me to see. Each was filled with a cloudy amber liquid. Something floated in the liquid, bouncing against the sides as Ku-Klip came closer. When he was inches from me he stopped and held them out so I could see.

The lumps inside the jars settled slowly to the bottom. I stared.

The talking head on the shelf was horrible. This was worse. Each jar held a perfectly preserved heart.

"When one creates a new body for someone, there are certain parts which do not have to be used. They can, in turn, be used as payment."

"You see, dear boy, I do not work for free."

"So you want my heart as payment?"

"Actually, I have no need for your heart. The two I have here have served me quite well. I have no need for another. However, there is something which perhaps you could help me acquire."

My heart, which had been racing, slowed a little now that it was certain it would remain with me. I cocked my head to one side. My eyes shot back to the thing still on the shelf. Ku-Klip followed my gaze. The head, still on its side, glared at us.

"No, boy, I have no need of your head. As you can see, I live humbly, so I have no need of your money, either."

I saw my chances slipping away.

"Then what do you want?'

"I want what was once mine."

Creak.

He undid my bindings at that point. Apparently he felt business negotiations should be done with a modicum of decorum. I should have ran while I had the chance.

"Do you know why I made the second Tin Man?" Ku-Klip continued without waiting for a response. "For the same reason I made the first. Fyter, like Chopper before him, fell in love with Nimmie Amee. Just like she had done with Chopper, the Wicked Witch cursed him. Limb by limb, he hacked himself to bits. Limb by limb, I replaced them with tin.

"It seemed a waste to dispose of those perfectly good limbs."

My stomach did a slow roll.

"As you have already deduced, I have more than a passing interest in the ways of magic. However, there is only so much that a lowly tinsmith can learn on his own. When the Witch was killed I saw my chance. I raided her house, taking everything I could. Spell books, instruments of magic, the glue I used to assemble the pieces of Chopper and Fyter into the man that Amee eventually married."

I felt a burning in the back of my throat. I swallowed hard to keep my bile down. I had heard rumors about Chopfyt, but had not believed them.

"The spell which allowed me to reanimate the dead flesh was from one of the Wicked Witch's grimoires. It was one of the easier spells, one of the ones I used to ease into the more difficulty magics. I had plans. I was going to be…"

His voice trailed off. His eyes took on a far away quality. I stole a look at the two jars on the table with the lumps of muscle floating in them. When I looked back at Ku-Klip I found his eyes boring into mine.

"What happened?" I asked, trying to hide the tremor in my voice.

"I was found out, that's what happened. Princess Ozma and that damn Woodsman took the Witch's possessions away from me. My own creation! I saved his life and he repaid me by betraying me. They said the knowledge was too dangerous for one man to possess."

The little Munchkin was pacing back and forth swinging his arms wildly.

"Too dangerous for me to possess is what they meant. The books, the glue, everything I took from the Wicked Witch's house is locked up with Ozma."

He spun to face me. His eyes gleamed. I felt myself withdraw involuntarily.

"That is how you can repay me."

I blinked, afraid to speak.

"I will make for you a new body. We can combine our knowledge, make you stronger than that Tin traitor. When you're ready you can march into Ozma's castle and take back what is mine."

His smile was full of cold anger.

"If you happen to run across the Woodsman in the process and have to kill him, well, I won't mind."

He smiled again and I knew why the Princess did not want him to have the knowledge held in the Wicked Witch's spell books. He was mad and his plan was insane and probably impossible. I looked back at the hearts resting on the table.

I started to form a plan of my own.

"Ku-Klip," I felt a smile of my own stretch my features. "You have a deal."

Creak.

That tiny cabin became my home. My whole world shrank until it consisted solely of Ku-Klip, his ramshackle house, and pain. The pain from the wasting disease was incredible. The pain of the process which Ku-Klip inflicted upon me was enough to make me forget the disease at times. Other times I silently begged to die.

We worked as quickly as we dared, constructing legs, arms, and a torso. Some were made of light tin. Other parts were gleaming steel. The legs were ready just in time. One day I woke to find I could do no more than sit upright. I could not bring my legs around. I could not stand, not even move my legs off of the thin bedding without using my hands.

That afternoon Ku-Klip took me outside, sat me on a scarred stump, and sawed off my legs.

The offending limbs had been dead to me all day. They were not, I soon found, dead to pain. I felt the teeth of the rusty saw bite into the flesh of my thigh. I stared as the skin split offering pink muscle to to blade. I screamed when the blood first pooled, then erupted skyward.

I lost consciousness.

When I came to I found that I my legs were still useless weights which I could not feel. I slid my hand beneath the thin blanket which covered my waist and felt something cold. I threw the thin cloth aside and beheld the bloody, gore caked metal which started a few inches below my hip. A pair of angry red lines marked the boundary where my flesh began and the metal started.

I lost consciousness again.

In the weeks that followed I learned many things. I learned that Ku-Klip had lived for centuries. He hinted that it had something to do with the information which he had acquired from the Wicked Witch. I learned that when necessary I could push myself past the point of exhaustion. I learned that I was a much better liar than I ever would have thought.

I learned that there were no limits to the pain which one person could endure.

Finally, the day came to complete the process. The shredded remnants of my body were starting to reject the metal limbs. Ku-Klip and I had completed the head and torso which I would soon inhabit. It was truly impressive. I would stand head and shoulders above any Munchkin I had ever met, taller even than the Woodsman himself.

I shaved my head in preparation for Ku-Klip's knife. The last thing he would do was transfer my brain from my dying body to my undying one. Then he would expect me to uphold my part of his plan. He had a rude surprise waiting. I had a plan of my own.

I lay outside on the ground. There was a thin blanket between me and the bare earth. Ku-Klip walked back and forth between the house and the operating area. He carried out knives, hammers, a saw, bandages. Next to these he placed a wand made of some twisted wood, a filthy bowl, other arcane items I did not recognize.

I tried not to fidget as he began chanting over me. Something moved at the edge of my peripheral vision. I tried to turn my head to see what it was but could not. Ku-Klip had given me tea which would put me into the trance state he needed for the spell to work. I thought I heard whimpering, but could discern little over the tinsmith's droning.

He the wand down and picked up a serrated knife. He motioned to whatever was standing off by the trees. Then he turned back to me.

"This may sting a little," he said.

I experienced two things almost simultaneously. The first was the shock which came with the knowledge that someone else was there. The crying I had heard, the movement I had seen, had been made by a young girl. The second was the eruption of pain as Ku-Klip slashed down. His knife severed my throat. I gasped but got no air. I felt the warm splatter of my own blood as it gushed up and fell back down to coat my face. I felt as if I was falling back into a long tunnel. Darkness swam in from all sides. As it washed over me I thought I heard another scream.

Creak.

I returned to consciousness in a panic. I could not breath, no matter how hard I tried. I opened my mouth to scream and heard nothing but the shriek of metal grinding on metal. Within seconds Ku-Klip was there. His cooed at me, trying to soothe me.

"Lie still, you are fine. Everything worked as it should."

He dipped a brush into the bowl, now filled with a dark liquid. He painted it along my lips, my jaw, the lower portion of my face. The stiffness began to ease. The viscous fluid loosened everything it touched.

"I can't breathe." I gasped.

"You don't need to. You no longer have lungs, a heart, a stomach. You no longer need to breathe or eat. This is all you need."

He streaked more of the stuff on me. I sat up stiffly.

"What is it?"

"Blood, of course."

I looked over to where I had laid down. My body was torn to pieces. I stared at my own face, slack, partially covered by a flap of my scalp. The top of my skull sat like an empty bowl.

Next to what had been my body for my whole life was another. It was the young Munchkin. Unlike my body, this one was almost perfectly intact. If not for the gash which opened the throat wide enough to allow me to see the spine behind it I would have thought her capable of sitting up and walking away.

"What have you done?"

Ku-Klip jumped in front of me. I stabbed at me with one finger. His whole hand was scarlet.

"I have done everything that you asked. I saved your life. Now you will do what I ask. Now you will keep your end of the bargain."

I answered him by swinging my metal arm hard into his midriff. He doubled over with a gasp. I struck him in the back of the head. My iron and steel hand connected with a loud crack.

"I will do no such thing," I said.

I strode over to the ruin of my body. I reached down with my new hands and cracked the ribs. I opened my old chest like a book. I slid one hand in and pulled out my heart. It came free with a tearing sound.

"I know your secret, wizard, tinsmith. You will not extend your own life at the expense of mine."

I threw my heart into the dirt. I stomped as hard as I could. The organ exploded beneath my metal foot. I strode past where Ku-Klip lay on the ground, stunned. I threw open the door of the house. With three quick strides I crossed to the cupboard.

The eyes in Chopper's head snapped open. I grabbed the hearts, one jar in each and, and threw them to to floor. Two more stomps reduced them to a paste which glittered with glass shards.

"What are you doing?"

It was Chopper, his head still sitting on the shelf.

"I am putting an end to you master. I have destroyed the hearts which kept him alive all these years as well as my own."

There is little in this world as unpleasant as the smile of a severed head.

"You idiot. It's not the hearts that keep Ku-Klip alive, it's the blood."

"The blood?"

"Yes, same as you."

I stood there for a moment, then ran out to where the three bodies lay in the dirt outside the house. Ku-Klip had rolled over. The ground beneath his head was slowly turning to mud as his life's blood drained into it. He was not dead yet, but would be soon.

"Traitor, just like the other," he gasped. "You have betrayed me."

"Not even your spells can keep you alive now."

He laughed until he chocked. A bubble of blood gurgled out of his mouth.

"And there is nothing which will keep you alive. No one else knows the secrets of the blood magic which animates that metal skin. That knowledge dies with me."

I felt panicked. Part of my mind wondered how I could feel this way without a heart beating in my chest.

"The Woodsman, Fyter, they know."

"Do you think either of them wants the world to know that they require blood to stay alive? They will destroy you for knowing their secret."

He laughed again, the gasped. His eyes lost their focus.

I stood there for a long time. Thoughts whirled through my mind, but I could not hold on to any of them for more than a moment. I needed blood to stay alive. I didn't know what to do with it, but I needed it. Ku-Klip was the only person who knew how to prepare the blood, there was no one else who would help me.

My head turned slowly to face the house. There was one other who knew the secret.

Creak.

The trick is never to allow yourself to get to the point where you need someone else to help you. Over time, the joints stiffen, the body freezes. It is almost like rigor mortis, but it does not go away over time. The only thing which will help is an application of the potion. It is not difficult to maintain, but it must be applied every few days. I can do this myself, if I have the chance.

What I did not know, was that it would wash away in the rain.

I stand, frozen, just a little off of the main road. I was on my way to confront the Woodsman. I have already gotten rid of Fyter. Ku-Klip was right about one thing. This secret is too large to share with others. I was on my way to Oz when I was caught in a downpour. The rain washed the blood magic from me and rooted me in place.

Fate has a cruel sense of humor. My traveling companion lies at my feet in a burlap sack. The limbless head is useless for this task. The blood has dried at my joints. It looks very much like rust. There is a can at my feet filled with a dark liquid, the blood potion. In the right light, it does look very much like oil.

I see how the Tin Man got away with his ruse all these years.

I am trapped here, a metal statue in the sun.

I am not worried. I am not far from the yellow bricks. The road to the Emerald City is well travelled. Sooner or later someone is bound to pass by. Some helpful stranger will come across me and my little "oil can."

They will provide me with everything I need.

Creak.

MR. PENNYWICKET'S TEA CUPS

"No I'm telling you we should have just left it in Devon. Bringing it with us is just inviting trouble."

"Leaving it there would be passing that trouble on to someone else."

"I got no problem with that."

Big Lem staggered as if the other man's words had knocked him back. He used his left hand to brush his long hair away from his face. His right found it's way into his pants pocket. He retrieved a worn purple rabbit's foot and began stroking it with his thumb.

"You don't mean that."

There was a long moment, then the pressure that had built up around the two men seemed to pop. Lem was suddenly aware of the noise surrounding them. The clanging of metal on metal, indiscernible orders shouted at a distance, gas powered generators roaring to life; the sounds came rushing in to fill the silence.

"Dale, you don't mean that." The "don't" was lower, more forceful.

"Lem," Dale sighed before continuing. The shame in his voice left the words muted. They still pierced Lem's heart.

"I think maybe I do mean exactly that."

Lem turned away, unable to endure the pain in his friend's eyes. He kept his back to Dale and let his words wash over him.

"I don't want anyone else to get hurt, Lem. You know I would never wish ill on anyone."

Lem stared out at the midway. He watched as it lumbered awake. Somewhere another generator was started. The demon on the facade of the Tunnel of Terror seemed to come to life as his eyes began to flow a fiery red. The corners of Lem's mouth twitched into a grin when he saw the tower of Devil's Drop snap vertical. Beyond that the spokes of the Ferris Wheel gleamed in the afternoon sun.

The games of Fast Chance Row were already in place. He knew that most of the newer help called it Fat Chance Row. He also knew that while all of the games were rigged in the house's favor, none of them were impossible to win. It was one of the things which separated Alistair Pennywicket's Traveling Amusements from so many of the other carnivals on the circuit.

That and the thing that they brought with them to every town they set up in.

"It's been fifteen years that we've been dragging it around. Why is it our burden to bear?"

Lem spun back to glare at Dale.

"Why? You know damn well why it is our burden to bear. Ours and no one else's."

"Then for God's sake let's tear it down. We can dismantle it. Leave a little bit at each stop this season. We can make sure it never hurts anyone again."

Lem wanted to give in to the pleading tone in his friend's voice. For all he knew Dale was right. They could strip the thing apart until it was nothing but sheet metal and loose bolts. Maybe that would work. Maybe that would be safe.

Or maybe each piece would act like the whole. Each tiny bit could be...infected with whatever dwelt in it now.

It was the old argument. They had been having it since the first night. They had been having it since before the first victim.

As long as Lem was Boss of the Midway they would play it safe. He was about to say so when a shrill voice pierced the air.

MR. PENNYWICKET'S TEA CUPS

"What is wrong with you people? School will be letting out in an hour and you are nowhere near ready. How do you expect to entice the darling little children with half built rides and semi-erect tents?"

The screech lost volume but not intensity as it moved away from where the two men stood. They heard the phrase "darling little children" spat out again. It was used so often that it had birthed its own acronym. DLC was whispered after the gates closed for the night, but never when there were any children present.

Certainly never when its creator was within earshot.

"I know what you were thinking, back in Devon."

Dale's voice was quiet. A note of sympathy tinted his words. Lem turned his attention back to Dale.

"We were all thinking it, hoping it had been long enough."

Dale glanced over at the conglomeration of steel and iron which comprised it. Despite the sunlight, it seemed to be enveloped in shadow. Even the stack of white cars appeared ominous.

Lem stared at it for the span of four breaths before replying.

"But it wasn't over, was it? It wasn't long enough? That's on us too. That little girl...just not enough."

"It is enough, Lem. That girl, her leg, that's not our fault. We did not know. Just like we did not know back then."

"I don't know that it will ever be enough."

Dale stabbed his right hand at Lem. The first two fingers pointed, accusing. The ring and little fingers were missing, along with a portion of his hand.

"How can you say we haven't paid enough? After everything? My hand. Billy."

Lem's eyes narrowed.

"Don't you dare mention him."

The color drained from Dale's face. He raised both hands, palms out. He made a patting, pacifying gesture. Lem could not help but follow the motion of the smooth scar tissue where the missing fingers should have been.

"I'm sorry to bring up your boy, but don't you see? All the blood, the lives ruined, the deaths; we should be square. It's taken too much for one little mistake."

Lem bristled again. Before he could rip into the 'little' comment, another voice joined the discussion.

"What in the holy Hell is going on over here? Lem? Why isn't this ride set up yet?"

The two men turned to see Richard Peterson, he of the DLC comment, stalking towards them. Peterson was the grandson of Alistair Peterson, known on the circuit as Alistair Pennywicket. He had taken over control of the carnival when the old man had finally passed away. Lem was the Midway Boss, but the Petersons were the owners. When Alistair had been alive he had the confidence in Lem to let him run the show. This was not the case with the younger Peterson.

The carnival had been a labor of love for Alistair. He lived to see the delight in the eyes of children, whatever their ages.

He understood that sometimes tragedies, even those caused by accident, could have long term repercussions. He would never do anything which might invite those repercussions.

Alistair Pennywicket had understood about the Tea Cups.

Richard Peterson was cut from a different cloth. He stepped in fresh from a job as Head of Acquisitions for some company out East. The suit he wore, the pant cuffs now stained by grass and splattered with mud from his tirade trip across the midway, belonged in a boardroom.

He belonged in a boardroom.

Unfortunately for everyone involved, he was taking his role as owner seriously. He was traveling with the show, overseeing everything. He had been with them for three of the longest months of Lem's life.

"Well, why isn't this even unpacked yet?"

"We're having a problem with..."

"There are some mechanical..."

Both Lem and Dale tried to answer at the same time. Lem had prepared a plausible lie which would keep the ride out of circulation for at least a little while. Peterson was ignorant of the actual nuts and bolts aspects of the individual attractions.

He did not get a chance to use it.

Peterson saw the look on Dale's face. His complexion darkened.

"Like Dale said, we're having a problem, a mechanical problem. It should be fixed in a few days, provided I can get the necessary parts."

"Elam Lundquist, do not lie to me. I've heard the rumors about the 'cursed ride.' Superstitious crap!"

"But sir..."

Peterson waved away Dale's protests.

"I don't care about the history of this ride."

He stared at each man in turn. There was no need for him to continue. It was obvious that he did not care about Dale's injury or the loss of Lem's son.

"What I care about is the present. What I care about is turning this ridiculous circus into a profitable organization. In order to do that I need every ride running."

He stepped up to the ride.

"Every ride. Even this one. Especially this one. For God's sake it's the Tea Cups! The darling little children will want to go on it again and again. They will whine until mommy and daddy pony up another handful of tickets."

He inhaled deeply. When he continued his voice was lower, but no less threatening.

"Mark my words, gentleman. You need to make sure that we can squeeze every dollar out of every family that walks through that gate. I'm not one of you traveling gypsy types. I'm a businessman. My job is to make sure that you turn a profit by the end of the year. If you don't I will dismantle this circus and sell it off piece by piece. Every attraction, every food stand, every game, every ride.

"Even this one."

He slapped the iron of the ride hard with the flat of his hand.

"Damn it!"

He snatched his hand away. There was a gash across his palm. A bright smear of blood stained the area he had touched.

"Jeez Mr. Peterson, that looks deep. Let me..."

Peterson pushed past Dale. He fumbled a handkerchief out of his pocket and pressed it against the wound. Within seconds it was soaked through.

"Out of my way. I have to disinfect this before I get blood poisoning."

Without another glance at the men or the ride, he headed off towards his personal trailer. Lem could see red drops fall from his hand to be soaked up by the bare earth. Halfway to his trailer he stumbled. Two steps later he staggered as if his legs would give out. He covered the remaining ground to his trailer in an uncoordinated rush. Both men could hear the door slam.

Lem and Dale glanced at each other, then at the Tea Cups. The spot where Peterson had hit the ride was bare. The crimson splash of Peterson's blood was gone. They looked at the trailer the owner had disappeared into. There was a long silence. Then Dale said what they were both thinking.

"Maybe we just got handed the solution to two problems at once."

"Not that you would ever wish ill on anyone."

Dale smirked.

"I maybe might could be persuaded to make an exception. Didn't Old Man Peterson say that if there were no family members to inherit the carnival would pass on to you?"

Dale walked away with a thoughtful smile.

Lem's own smile only lasted for a few seconds. If he took over he wouldn't only be responsible for the carnival, he would own it. Every attraction, every food stand, every game, every ride; all his.

Even the Tea Cups.

HOLDING

John Highgart strode quickly down the hallway. His crepe soled shoes whispered over the think carpeting. The doors he passed on either side were made of wood polished until they seemed to gleam with their own light. There were small numbered signs affixed to the wall to the right of each door. The numbers were all they contained, no names, no descriptions, just the room number.

"John Highgart to Conference Room 14B. John Highgart to Conference Room 14B."

The voice issuing from above was completely neutral. It seemed neither male nor female. The carefully modulated words gave no indication of why John should report to Conference Room 14B, only that he should do so.

It was only the second time he had been summoned anywhere since he had arrived at the compound -- how long ago? Had it been years? It seemed like it had been years, then again, it didn't.

That he had been sent for seemed important. Was he in some kind of trouble? Had he transgressed somehow and would be expelled?

Was he finally being allowed to move on, to leave the holding area?

There was no way to know. Good or ill, he would find out soon enough. John reached 14B, the gilded numbers sparkling under the lights. Double doors separated the hall from the room. He paused and tried to control his breathing. Eyes closed, he raised his hand and knocked on the right hand door.

The door opened slowly, silently. Before his eyes could adjust to the difference in lighting, a voice called out to him.

"John, please come in."

John Highgart stepped quietly into the room. The door closed behind him.

A long, slightly curved table occupied the bulk of the room. The table top was a deep reddish wood with blonde wood trim around its edge. The chairs which encircled the table were made of the same light wood. Their cushions matched the red of the table top.

The speaker rose from where he sat at the far end of the table.

"John, I am so glad you are here. We were starting to get worried."

We?

John glanced around but saw no one else.

"I'm sorry, George. I got a little turned around. This is the first time I have ever heard my name being broadcast."

He pointed a finger upward. The announcement had stopped. John shrugged. George smiled and shook his head. His long blond hair flowed for a moment, then was still.

"No need to apologize, John. As for the announcement, it should be the last time you hear your name being broadcast as well as the first."

"Do you mean?"

George's smile broadened.

"Yes, everything is finally ready. You have been in holding for a long time but all of that is behind you now. The time of your Transition has arrived."

The importance he bestowed upon the word implied a capital T.

John sagged visibly. He caught himself on the edge of the table, his arms quivering as he fought to hold himself upright. George hurried to his side. A stringless puppet, John allowed himself to be guided into a chair. George moved him gently to the center of the table where the curve was most pronounced. This was comforting. The reassuring stability of the wooden table top was not only in front of him, but a little on either side as well.

"Steady there," George said. He remained at John's side until he was certain that he was not going to pitch forward or faint and slide out of the chair.

"It's just," John began.

"I know." George reclaimed his seat at the opposite end of the table.

"It's been so long. I mean, it seems like it has been a long time. It also seems like no time at all has passed."

"It has been seventy-three years."

"What?"

"Seventy-three years, a long time indeed. A very long time to remain in holding."

"That's just it, the holding part. That's what made it so bad, not knowing where I was or where I would be going."

John trailed off, not wanting to complete the sentence, not wanting to ask the question. Although he was dying for the answer, he feared it more. George's smile and calm demeanor did little to assuage his fear. George probably dealt with this all of the time.

"All of your questions will be answered soon enough, my friend. There are just a few things which need to be addressed before you can complete your Transition."

"The bureaucracy of the afterlife?"

"Something like that, yes." George looked over his shoulder. There was a door there, a door which John had not noticed until George looked at it. It was a single door, smaller than either of the pair John had used to enter the room.

"We would like to apologize for the delay in processing your Transition. There are certain matters which must be attended to before you can be allowed to move on, matters which require…"

A soft rapping at the door interrupted George. Before he could say anything else, the door opened.

"Excuse me, we are not quite ready here, yet."

"I have waited as long as I am going to," the intruder said. She was a tiny thing, no more than five feet tall, slender.

Splatters of dried blood marked her face, neck, and arms.

John snapped back in his seat. The woman approached him, arms outstretched.

"Don't you pull away from me, Johnny Highgart. Don't you dare pull away from me again."

There was something about her voice which sparked a memory. John stared at the bloodied woman, tried to see passed the bruises, mottled skin.

"Annie?"

Memories flooded in on him. Images of Annie, alive, vibrant, long strawberry blonde hair flowing behind her as she ran up a hill somewhere. Another image, the light dimmer, the sky a blaze of red and orange. Dawn or dusk, John wasn't sure. Annie's eyes sparkling, full of mischief.

John was just starting to smile when the image changed again. This time it was a different Annie, her cheeks blotchy, her eyes red rimmed. No sound accompanied the flashbacks, but John did not need any. He remembered the moment vividly. He remembered Annie's anguished wails, her denials, and her repeating "why" over and over. He remembered his own murmured explanations, platitudes so overused that they were insulting.

The next image which slammed into his mind was not memory. It was one he could never have seen. An overhead view showed a small knot of young people, teenagers, including a much earlier version of himself. They were all dressed in their best clothes, suits and dresses for some, jeans and sweaters for others. They were milling about on a hillside beneath a dark sky which threatened rain.

Suddenly John knew why this visitor looked the way she did. The teens in the last image were mourners at a funeral.

Annie's funeral.

John's sight returned to him. Annie stood before him. Only the table kept her from coming closer. Her arms were raised over her head. The blood pattern made sense this way. The droplets which marred her face and neck matched tracks which ran down her arms, starting at her wrists. Those wrists were hacked open, deep cuts bisecting them. One long gash ran down the inside of her left arm. The wounds were ragged. The flesh was cut in some places, torn in others.

"I didn't have time to get a knife," Annie said in a quiet voice. "I finished the bottle, then smashed it and used the broken glass. I needed to do it before I changed my mind."

She held out her arms again. Her fingertips missed grazing John's face by less than an inch.

"The funny thing is that I did change my mind. I tried to slow the bleeding by holding my arms above my head, just like they taught us in health class. I can't believe I remembered it at the time, but then, I always did really well in school.

"I did better with the glass."

Annie was looking at the gashes in her arms. She slowly raised her gaze to meet John's. He wanted nothing more than to turn away, but he couldn't. Annie's eyes were cold, hard. When she spoke again, her voice was just as cold, just as hard.

"I loved you," she said quietly. The words were more an accusation than a declaration of her feelings. John flinched.

"I loved you."

Her voice was louder, shriller. She began to keen, a horrible banshee wail which cut deep into John. He tried to speak, tried to find something to say, but could only manage a squeak.

Annie's eyes flared once more. Then she burst apart. Her body seemed to glow for a minute, then disintegrated in a shower of bright golden sparks. Her wail was cut off by a 'pop' and a rush of air.

The room was suddenly silent.

John sat there stunned. He stared at the place where the bloodied corpse of his first real girlfriend had stood just seconds before. He looked down at his trebling hands. Then he looked up at George.

"Just what the hell is going on here?" he shouted. He tried to rise to his feet, but his legs would not support him. He fell back into the chair. It slid, carrying him backwards until he bumped into the wall.

George looked back over his shoulder at the door which Annie had come through. He glanced quickly at John, then down. John could have sworn he saw a red flush creeping up the other's neck.

"Ah yes, that was the thing which I wanted to speak to you about before."

"That was the thing? That my dead ex-girlfriend was going to come and pay me a visit?"

"Well, yes, among others."

John stared at him.

"Others?"

"Yes, if you had arrived earlier I would have had a chance to explain the process before it began."

"Process? What process? I've been here for God knows how long, stuck in some kind of weird Limbo or something. No one will tell me where I am or how long I will be here, where I am going or even if there is a somewhere to go to. Now you're telling me that there is a process?"

"All of this could have been explained, earlier, yes. However, we find that doing so causes undue stress upon our guests."

"So you kept me in the dark out of kindness, you didn't want me to experience 'undue stress.'"

George brightened.

"Yes, that's it exactly."

"You obviously have a less than perfect grasp of the concept of sarcasm," John muttered. George, if he had heard the words, ignored them. He continued on.

"As I mentioned earlier, before our first guest arrived, there are a few things which must be addressed before your Transition can be completed. The most important of these is The Audience."

"The Audience," John repeated. "I take it that was The Audience?"

He pulled himself upright in the seat, took a deep breath, then exhaled slowly. At least the worst part was over.

"Oh no, The Audience is not a single meeting. It is a process. That is why you have had to wait so long. We had to wait for everyone else to arrive. Poor Annie has been waiting even longer than you."

John shrank back down in his chair.

"Everyone?"

"Everyone you wronged, yes. Everyone with whom you interacted over the course of your life whose experience was somehow diminished by their encounter with you."

"Everyone?"

"Well, no, not everyone." George chuckled. "We can't have *everyone* you ever encountered traipsing through here. That would take forever. Nothing would ever get done. We would have a serious overcrowding problem.

"No, I misspoke. I should have said everyone with whom you had a long and meaningful relationship who was harmed or hurt by you or by their relationship with you."

"So everyone I loved, or who," he paused, thinking about Annie," or who loved me?"

"Yes, but not just romantic relationships. All those with whom you had meaningful interactions. In fact," George titled his head. There was a knock at the door.

"In fact here is the next one now."

John wanted to get up and leave. He tried to stand, but he could not get his legs to move. Before he could overcome his sudden weakness, the door opened.

It had taken a few seconds for John to recognize Annie. It had been decades since he had seen her. Decades while he had been living. That wasn't counting the time since he had died. There was no such difficulty recognizing Brian. He looked exactly as he had the last time John had seen him.

Well, perhaps not exactly. Brian had always been lean, but now he was thin to the point of looking gaunt. His close cropped hair was more salt than pepper. Once he had towered over everyone in the room. Now he walked stooped over, his steps slow and careful.

The most startling difference was his clothing. When they had worked together, Brian had always been the sharpest dresser in the office. Even among those who 'dressed to impress,' Brian stood out. The man shuffling slowly into the room was not clothed in a silk suit and tie. Instead he wore faded brown slacks, one cuff trailing threads. His shirt, once white but now faded to a beige non-color, was buttoned up to his neck. The collar of the shirt was frayed. A well worn cardigan was wrapped around him. The sweater would have fit a man a few sizes larger. On Brian it was huge, enveloping him in gray wool.

The hair, the clothing, the stoop all combined to create the impression of a very old man.

John was taken aback. He had been older, at least older than he appeared now, when he had arrived here. Within days he looked and felt as he did now. He assumed that it worked the same for everyone else. If you had the option of looking and feeling whatever age you wanted to, why would anyone choose to look like this?

Of course, if that were true, why did Annie look as she did? Did she choose to appear how she did immediately after death forever ?

John knew what he saw when he looked in a mirror, but not what he looked like to other people.

A cold spike of fear planted itself firmly in his stomach.

John was startled out of his rumination by motion on the other side of the table. He looked up at Brian, of the shell of the person who had been Brian. Dark, watery eyes stared out of the gaunt face. John endured their gaze for what seemed like hours before finally breaking down.

"I'm sorry, Brian. I am so sorry."

Brian stood there, unmoving.

"For the ad campaign, for not giving you the credit you deserved, all of it. I mean, I didn't know that they would be letting people go only weeks later. Who can predict that kind of thing? If I had known that stupid commercial was the only thing keeping either of us alive there I would have made sure that they knew how much work you put into it. It could have just as easily been me laid up with the flu and you making the pitch. Would it have changed things? Who knows?"

The old man who had once been his best friend and business partner blinked once.

"I...I'm sorry."

John's head dropped. He could not tolerate the stare any longer. He heard a slow shuffling. When he looked up he saw that Brian was halfway across the room.

"Brian, wait," he said to the other's retreating back. Brian did not stop, did not slow. There was no indication that he had even heard. He continued his slow path back towards the door he had entered through. As he did, he became less 'there' somehow. At first John was not sure, but after a few seconds he was certain that he could see through his old partner. Brian was becoming less substantial the further he got from John. It took much longer for Brian to cross the room this time. He never did make it to the door. He was still a good six feet away when he faded completely. This was accompanied by the same pressure releasing "pop" which had occurred when Annie vanished, but there were no pyrotechnics. Brian simply dissolved.

He did so without speaking a single word to John. He did not even turn around to see him one last time.

John sat there, his heart heavy in his chest. He had not thought about Brian for years. Once he had felt horribly guilty, yet he had never done anything for his friend. He told himself that it would not have mattered. He told himself that Brian was a big mover in the business who would get back on his feet in no time. He certainly did not need John's help.

So John never returned his calls. After a few months of avoiding Brian, it became easier to do. He convinced himself that he had done nothing wrong. When, years later, he heard about Brian's financial troubles, he did so without an ounce of remorse.

He felt that remorse now.

There was another knock at the door which made John groan. It opened to admit a stunningly attractive young woman. She had not aged at all since the last time John had seen her. In fact, she looked to be about the age she had been when they first met. She flipped her head with a practiced move that caused her long, auburn hair to become airborne for a brief moment. It settled to frame her face perfectly. Her eyes were green. They narrowed for a moment when she first saw John. Although he could not see them from where he sat, he knew that there were little flecks of gold floating in her irises.

Her too red lips twisted into something that was part smile, part sneer. She arched an eyebrow.

"John."

Her voice was both melodious and frighteningly frigid. With one word she both acknowledged and dismissed him.

"Karrie," John tried for the same disinterested tone but failed. It was difficult to act removed when the scenes of the two of them were playing out in his mind. Little flirtatious looks were replaced by the two of them together. Gentle kisses, stolen touches. As before the view was one John could never have had. From outside himself he saw them in cars, hotel rooms, her apartment, even in his own house once when his wife was visiting her dying mother.

John closed his eyes hard, but the images would not stop. Every time the two of them writhed around flashed into his memory. They were quickly replaced by other scenes: the two of them at lunch, suddenly uncomfortable with each other. Two people, once close, but who no longer knew how to relate to each other. He saw himself crying, yelling, crying again.

"What?" he hollered. "How the hell did I ever hurt you?"

The half sneer was replaced by a look of startled amusement. They eyebrow remained raised.

"I only wanted to be with you! I was going to give it all up for you. My wife, the house, everything. I never hurt you. You left me. You ruined my life."

"Really?" Karrie asked in a voice that dripped like warm honey.

"Yes, really. Tell me what I did to you. Tell me the one thing that, what was it he said, diminished your life?"

John stabbed a finger at George, then at Karrie. George seemed surprised by this outburst and leaned back in his chair a little. Karrie only pursed her lips, shook her head, and leaned closer.

"What did you do? You made me doubt myself, that's what you did. For years we snuck around and you told me how you were going to leave it all for me, how one day we would be together. You never did, did you? Oh, you left your wife, eventually. You finally got up off of your ass and went out to find your bliss or whatever, but you didn't do it for me, did you? You never did it for me."

"You left me," John repeated. The words were quiet, filled with the sting of ancient rejection.

"I didn't leave you. I couldn't leave you. We were never really together. All I could do was stop seeing you. You can't leave someplace you've never been."

Karrie leaned even closer. A hint of vanilla wafted over to John. The green eyes bore down on him. They gleamed in the light, shimmered, but the tears they held never fell.

"What did you do to me? You made me feel like I wasn't good enough. You made me doubt myself. You made me feel worthless."

Her voice was hard and full of contempt.

"You want to know the one thing that you did that 'diminished my life?' You walked over and said hello."

She turned on one heel. Her back to him, she drew a deep breath. Without looking, she spoke over her shoulder. John could see her hair caught behind one ear.

"I loved you once. I hated you for a long time. Now I just don't care."

There was a shower of sparks, a flash so brilliant that it left spots dancing before John's eyes, and the 'pop' he had come to expect. There was a moment of peace while the pressure in the room stabilized. The John erupted.

"What the hell is this?" He shouted his question at the ceiling. George shrank further back in his chair.

"Is this some sick version of This is Your Life? This WAS Your Life? Where's Ralph Edwards?"

"He made his Transition a few years ago."

"What?"

George's face was calm. He titled his head to one side. When he spoke, his voice was calm, soothing, and without any trace of the nervousness he had displayed just moments before.

"Mr. Edwards completed his Transition years ago. Despite all of the happiness he brought to people, he too had his time in your seat. Well, not that seat exactly, but you understand my meaning."

"I understand your meaning but I don't understand all of this."

"I know it is difficult to come to grips with. The process is a bit," he paused, looking for the right word, "unbalanced."

"Unbalanced."

"Yes, it is a trifle unfair to make one relive all of the disappointments, all of the hurt, all of the negative portions of ones life without experiencing the joys and triumphs again. Believe me, when we are done here and The Transition is complete you will understand."

"So there's more? Of course there's more. Stupid question John. So, who's next?"

John started to make a flippant comment as he turned towards the door. Movement at the edge of his vision stopped him. Standing in the center of the room were his wife and daughter.

"How?" he sputtered. The door had not opened. They had not entered the room. They had just appeared.

Of course, Annie and Karrie had just disappeared, why couldn't others just appear?

"Lori."

His wife, ex-wife actually, looked haggard. Her hair was disheveled. There were dark circles under her eyes. She chewed on her lower lip, something she did when she was unsure of herself.

John looked from her to their daughter. While Lori appeared to be somewhere in her mid to late forties, well after the divorce, Sylvie looked like he was eight, maybe nine years old.

That was wrong. If Lori was in her forties, then Sylvie should be in her teens. She had been in her thirties when John had died. She was a doctor with her own practice, happily married with two children of her own.

Of course, he had never met either of his grandchildren. He had not even been invited to the wedding.

Eyes closed, John waited for the images to appear. He expected more of what he had seen before: external views of himself and the people whose lives he had damaged. What he saw instead were pudgy little hands. They were holding a red block. In the background he could hear his own voice yelling, Lori's voice responding, even louder. The words were indistinguishable, but the tone was clear.

The image shifted quickly. The sounds were the same, or at least similar, yelling. Now the view was nothing but fluffy white fur and darkness. A smell came to him, filling his nostrils. It was the green grass and kibble smell of Mr. Perkins, their first dog.

Realization crashed into John. He was not simply experiencing the moments again, he was experiencing them from Sylvie's view. She was a little girl, hiding under her bed while her parents raged at each other in another room. She had dragged the dog under the bed with her for comfort.

Back in the conference room, John began to cry.

Another scene, still from the viewpoint of his little girl. Through her eyes he saw himself climbing into a car filled with cardboard boxes. From the window he watched himself drive away. He felt an ache, a longing, and knew that Sylvie was trying not to cry, not to cry out. He knew that she wanted to run after him, beg him to take her with him. He knew that Lori was standing right there, also staring out of the window.

"Daddy."

One word.

It was all that was needed to convey the sense of abandonment, longing, despair, anger, doubt, and guilt which Sylvie had lived with from that moment on. John knew why Sylvie appeared to be eight years old. There was a part of her which had never grown any older, a part which remained a sad, scared, emotionally scarred little girl.

"Sylvie, I am so sorry. It was never because of you. It me and your mom, we just, tell her Lori."

When he looked up at his ex-wife he saw that she had changed. Her once brown hair was now grey and thinning. Deep lines marred her face. The hand with which she held Sylvie's was old and wrinkled.

"Lori? You're old. You, oh. I see. This must be how you looked."

John trailed off as he looked at his little girl.

"Sylvie, if you are here then you must be." He could not complete the sentence. He closed his eyes, unable to look at his daughter, knowing how badly he hurt her.

John sat, head in his hands, waiting for the images to assault him. Would it be the horrible screech followed by the crushing pain of a car accident? Perhaps constant pain as cancer slowly devoured her.

Minutes passed with no views of Sylvie's death. John opened his eyes to find himself alone with George. He had not heard the pop, felt the release of pressure.

"Where?" he asked.

"Gone," George answered. "Through the door."

"How?"

"I'm afraid that is not for you to know, now."

"But I saw,"

"You saw the moments which brought her pain, yes. You know when she was thinking about you."

"So in the end?"

George did not answer. He did not need to. Throughout her life, John had been a source of sorrow and pain, yet at the end she had not thought of him at all. He tried to imaging this as a good thing, that she had died suddenly and without pain. Maybe she had died surrounded by those who loved her.

There was a knock at the door.

THE REST OF THE AFTERNOON, if that was how long they were in the conference room, was a blur. John endured what seemed like an endless stream of people. Some yelled at him, some cried, some said nothing at all. None of them really mattered. Their pains were tiny additions to the soul crushing anguish he had caused Sylvie. His daughter, the one person he should have cared for more than any other.

Nothing else mattered. John sat there numb as the people paraded through.

Then they were done.

A few minutes had passed before John realized that no one had come through the door in some time. He looked over at George who was smiling beatifically.

"That is it, my friend. This part of the process is over."

"No more people?"

"No more."

"So now what? I stay here, trapped with the knowledge of how I hurt all of these people? I get to sit here with all of their pain trapped inside me? I was right all along, this is Hell."

"No, no," George said, rising and walking over to John. "Not at all, this is only Holding."

He touched John's shoulder, biding him to stand. George supported him as he stood, weak, physically drained after his ordeal. He was too weak to protest as George began leading him towards the door.

"So what happens now?"

"Now you complete The Transition."

They were closer now, only a few steps away from the door.

The door which all of his tormentors had come through.

"No, no. I don't want to face them all again. I don't want these memories. Don't make me go see them again."

George shushed him, patted his shoulder.

"Oh, no, you misunderstand. You will not have the memories. You are going to make your Transition."

He reached for the doorknob. John tried to hold back. A firm hand on his shoulder kept him from pulling away.

"You must endure the process so you understand the pain you have caused in your past life. Now, you must seek to undo that pain. You must be better this time. You must be kinder, love more, strive to put others before your own desires."

George turned the handle. The door wrenched open. There was a roar of wind. John could see brilliant colors swirling and nothing else. There was no floor, no walls, nothing. There was only the void and the colors and the ceaseless howling wind.

"What do you mean 'this time'?" John had to scream to be heard over the wind. His hair whipped about his face.

"This time, this life. You are about to complete your Transition."

John felt George's hand leave his shoulder. It was pressed firmly against his back.

"You are about to be reborn."

John tried to turn, to look at George, to try to determine if what he was saying was true. He tried to turn away from the horrible beauty of the swirling colors.

"In each life we meet the same people," George said. His voice was even, but John still heard the words booming in his head, even over the wind coming through the door.

"As you live, you will once again meet all of the people you wronged in this life. They will not be the same people, will not look the same. Just as you will be someone new, someone who looks nothing like John Highgart. You will not have the memories of this life, as you have no memories of your past lives.

"However, you will meet the same souls. Your souls will know each other. If you treat them well, better than you did, then the process will be shorter next time. Each rebirth is a chance to live better. Each life is a chance to stop the process altogether.

"Good luck, John Highgart. Live well."

He pushed John through the doorway.

The wind tore at him, slammed him. John was battered, although there was nothing solid. The colors swirled around him, a maddening array. He felt as if he were falling yet there was no sense of gravity.

As he fell, John Highgart realized that Holding was neither Heaven nor Hell. Hell was the experience. Hell was reliving all of the pain over again. Hell was the chance to make things right, without the knowledge of what or why.

He screamed.

His shriek was the incoherent outpouring of all of his fear and anguish.

He could not breath. The colors were invading him, the wind denying him air.

Suddenly he could breath again. There was a bright light. Blurry images swam through his vision. He filled his lungs and wailed.

The wail of a newborn infant.

ELLA

Everything was always the same. The same hard floor, the same cold hearth, the same rotted food, the same dirt, the same filth.

"Anastasia, call your sisters for dinner."

"Yes mother." The attractive young woman smiled at her mother before walking out of the kitchen and down the hallway towards the front door. The house, as always, was spotless. The wooden floors gleamed a warm honey yellow. The walls were white, not tan, not beige, but gleaming white. This was quite a feat when one lived at the end of a long dirt road.

The hallway ended at the front door with a stair case on either side. The one on the left led up to the small bedrooms. Anastasia cupped her hand to her mouth and called out.

"Druzella, dinner is ready."

She then turned to face the second stair way. This one led down to the cellar. The light from the hallway illuminated only the first few steps before being swallowed up by the darkness. Anna hated the cellar. She dreaded having to go down to fetch preserves from the little shelves at the bottom of the stairs. The orange glow of the central fireplace brought to mind the gates of hell itself.

She knew that she would never be able to stay down there for more than a few minutes at a time. She did not understand how anyone could. It was frightening enough to shatter one's sanity.

"Elinora." Her voice was much quieter than when she had called her sister. "Elinora, Mother says that the food is almost ready."

Anastasia stared into the gloom for another few seconds, then hurried back down the hall to the warmth and brightness of the kitchen. She tried to tell herself that her quick steps were caused by nothing more than her hunger.

Ella remembered a time when things were different. She remembered a wonderful time when both of her parents had been alive. She remembered the sun warm in the sky. She remembered the cool breezes off the lake which made up the southern boundary of their land. She remembered the grass beneath her bare feet.

She remembered her mother's sickness. She remembered the horrible wet cough which never seemed to get any better. She remembered her mother to breath, betrayed by her own body. Her mother, once beautiful, had aged somehow. Her skin, so pale that it was almost translucent, became mottled and gray.

Ella remembered taking turns with the brush. First she would brush her mother's hair. When her little arms tired she would relinquish the brush. Her mother would brush Ella's hair in long, smooth strokes. One hundred strokes, every night. Ella almost always fell asleep before her mother reached the half-way point.

Her blonde hair, so like Ella's, lost its luster and finally its color, turning first dull, then gray, then it began to fall out by the handful.

She had been a very young girl when her mother died. Ella watched helpless as it became harder and harder for her mother to breathe. Finally, it was too difficult and her mother gave up.

Hardly more than a child, she had to take over the duties of the mistress of the house.

ELLA

At least for a little while.

Her mother's death had been a horrible, prolonged ordeal for the young Ella. The few months which followed had been sad, but they had been peaceful. The years which had followed after her father had met the witch had been longer and more terrible than anything she could have imagined.

"This is better than anything I could have imagined for you."

The food sat, uneaten, forgotten, on the sideboard. Their mother smiled at the two girls from her place by the front door. Druzella sat on the Ottoman. Her hands were folded primly in her lap. She sat with her back perfectly straight, her knees close together. Her sister, on the other hand, was pacing the floor between her sister and her mother. Anxious, skittish, inconstant, so unlike her sister.

Anastasia was the more attractive of the pair, but Druzella would make a better match someday. It looked as if that day could be very soon.

Their visitor had swooped in and then left. He had remained just long enough to make his announcement, then swept off again. In his wake he left a whirlwind of dreams and desires. None of them could believe it, least of all the girls' mother. A royal ball, with all of the court in attendance. A bevy of women of marrying age from which the Prince would choose his bride.

There would be respectable young ladies there. Her daughters would pale next to the daughters of count and dukes, the progeny of the landed gentry. Still, perhaps they could catch the eye of someone while they were there. Perhaps a dance could turn into a courtship which could lead to marriage. Imagine, her daughters married to a great landowner. Imagine, never having to worry about the crops, the servants, her own future.

Imagine, one of her girls, married to a prince.

Anastasia's voice pulled her back from her fantasies.

"I am sorry." Anastasia's face fell when she heard her mother's response. The older woman waited patiently for her daughter to repeat her question. Instead she stood where she had stopped her pacing. Her pink bow of a mouth was parted slightly, her blue eyes wide.

Yes, her looks would have to be enough to attract a suitor. She had precious little else to offer.

"I am sorry, Anna. I did not hear your question. Would you be kind enough to repeat yourself for your aging mother and her failing ears?"

The relief on the girl's face was evidence that she had missed the sarcasm in her mother's request.

"Are we to go to the ball?" Tremors of anticipation washed over the girl. Druzella leaned almost imperceptibly forward in her chair.

"Of course. We will all go to the ball."

Relief washed over the girls. After a moment, Druzella's face darkened. Her brow wrinkled. Her mouth turned down. The girl spoke before her mother could reproach her or remind her about lines and wrinkles.

"All of us?" she asked.

"Yes, of course all of us. It would be unseemly for the two of you to be presented to the court without a proper escort. It would be better if your escort was a gentleman, but I will have to make do."

"No…" Druzella paused, then corrected herself. "Excuse me, Mother. I was not asking if we three would be going, I was asking if we would all be going."

"Yes, all of us," a note of exasperation crept into her voice.

"All of us, even Ella?"

―――

She could hear them murmuring and muttering upstairs. Something had happened which had set the whole household into a flurry of motion. There had been a long discussion in the great room. Someone, probably flighty Anna, had been pacing across the floor for what seemed like hours. It had nearly driven Ella mad, clop clop clop, right over her head. She took satisfaction in knowing that such unladylike behavior had probably driven her step-mother just as crazy.

After an eternity or two they had all headed upstairs. It sounded like a herd of cattle navigating the stairs. Ella could picture the head witch driving her daughters before her.

They had retired to their chambers earlier than usual. They had not retired for the night. Despite the space between them, Ella could still hear the other three bustling about in the upper rooms. She could hear them talking, but could not make out the words. From the inflections and exclamations each of her step-sisters had been alternately excited, appalled, and finally appeased.

Ella waited for her step-family to come back down to the main floor. Surely someone would come down eventually, to extinguish the lamp in the kitchen if for no other reason. She waited and waited down in the gloom. A pale golden glow illuminated the crack between the floor and the bottom of the door.

Eventually the sounds which had drifted down to her ceased. Ella crept to the bottom of the stairs. Her head was cocked to one side, an animal seeking sound, desperately trying to sense its surroundings. She felt like a small animal, perhaps one of the huge rats which she shared her living space with. She was both predator and prey, seeking sustenance but ever alert for the movement of something further up the food chain.

She pressed her against the stairs. She stared at the light which still spilled beneath the sill. It both attracted and repulsed her. She knew how the night-flyers felt. The little moths were drawn irresistibly to the flickering flames of candle and lamp, despite the dangers they possessed.

Ella raised one hand, held it before her for a moment, then brought it gently down upon the riser before her. She repeated the process with the other hand, with first one foot, then the other. She moved this way, the slow crawl of a crab. She waited between each movement, testing the quality of the silence above her, before moving again.

The door opened silently, its hinges well oiled. Ella glanced up. The staircase leading to the bedchambers was dark. There was no sign of life save the quiet snoring of one of the girls. Another small imperfection for her step-mother to worry about, another small smile from Ella.

The hallway and the dining area were cloaked cloaked in gray shadows. Ella was accustomed to the darkness. Living under the stairs, only coming out at night to sweep and clean, had given her a healthy appreciation for the gloom. Shadows could hide young girls from the taunts of wicked step-mothers. Shadows could hide young girls from the cruel tricks of evil step-sisters. Shadows were Ella's friends, much as were the rats which shared her living space by the fireplace in the basement.

The light, however, was not something to which Ella was accustomed. She paused at the threshold of the kitchen. The lamp cast shadows, true, but the way which it illuminated the room caused Ella to squint. Her eyes flicked from one surface to the next--the water basin, the sideboard still stacked high with the evening meal, the black iron stove, now cold. She was used to doing her work by the light of its embers. Tonight she had the light of the lamp.

First, the food. Ella fell upon the meal like a thing starved, for a thing starved was her nature. There was so much that was missing from her life. So much of her world had gone dark the day father married the monstrosity which now slept in his chambers.

The cold mutton stuck in her gullet. Thoughts of her new family caused her throat to constrict. She set the food aside and began to clean.

How three women, especially three women who aspired to be ladies, could reduce a house to shambles in one day was something beyond Ella's ken. Still, the proper role of a dutiful daughter was to keep a clean house. She would never consider herself daughter to the hag who slept upstairs. It was not for that woman's benefit that she cleaned, although the three who lived in her father's house certainly benefited from her nightly cleaning. It was because of her father's memory that she cleaned. She would not allow his house to fall into ruin.

She scrubbed and scoured, swept and sponged. The lamp in the kitchen guttered and went dark. Ella was used to the darkness. It did not stop her movements. She cleaned until the house was spotless, until all traces of her step-family had been erased. By dawn, she was finished. From the kitchen she removed half of a loaf of bread and an apple. These would sustain her down in the cellar while the coven roamed through the house, putting their foul stink on everything again.

The first light of morning stole in through the window. Ella hurried down the hall. Although she desperately wanted to retreat to the safety of her rooms, she spied two things which made her pause.

The first was the window set in the wall next to the door. Through it, Ella could see the tree which grew in front of the house. Many years ago her parents would sit beneath that tree, reading and singing to infant Ella. She had no memory of this, but it was a tale her father told her many times after her mother had died.

Ella's eyes watered. Her focus shifted from what was beyond the window to the window itself. Glass was terribly expensive. The glazed window in the front of the house was a sign of her father's prosperity. Few could afford the luxury of being able to see what was outside while still maintaining a barrier between that which was in and that which was out.

She sunlight gleamed on the glass. The angle of the rising sun caused the window to become opaque. Instead of showing her what was outside, it provided a reflection of all that was inside.

Ella stood, eyes wide, struck by the horror that was revealed. Staring back at her was a gangly girl, all elbows and angles. The gray cloth of her dress hung from emaciated shoulders. The shapeless garment hid her thin body. He face was streaked with grime. Her hair, once the focus of a mother's love, was tangled and dusted with soot.

She turned away from the horrible vision of herself. She wanted to run down the stairs, but stopped abruptly. There was a small table next to the door. It was a holdover from the days when her father would entertain company. The guest would announce their arrival by placing cards printed with their names on the table. After the guests had left, her mother would use these cards as a record of who had attended.

There had been no such gatherings since the death of her father. The table had gone unused for years. Until now.

The creak of a floorboard shattered Ella's reverie. She looked up the stairs. The creak was followed by footfalls. One of the women was awake and moving around. Without thinking, Ella snatched the parchment from the table and slipped through the doorway to the cellar. She eased the door closed. She waited until the owner of the footfalls had started down the stairwell. Ella matched her steps to the steps moving from the upper floor to the main floor. She reached the hard packed dirt of the cellar floor and ran to the far wall. She huddled against the corner, shivering, as the house began its new day above her.

THE HOUSE WAS a study in barely controlled chaos. Anastasia was practically beside herself. She was desperate to find a gown which would show her in the best light. Her anxiety was infectious. By mid-afternoon her mother was barely able to concentrate on her own needlework. Even Druzella, always the picture of tranquillity was beginning to show signs of distress.

The older woman looked at her daughters and sighed. The house was already in a state and the ball was still days away. She could only imagine how things would deteriorate as the evening of the ball drew closer. The girls, and she had to admit, she herself, would get more and more excited.

A BALL! How exciting! Ella read the parchment by the amber glow of the coals as she stoked the main fireplace. This could be her opportunity to escape the grasp of her step-mother. Better still, perhaps she could combine her lineage with that of one of the finer families of the realm. Then she could escape the drudgery of her life but not lose the home which she had known her whole life.

She turned the page towards the fire again, angling it so she could best make out the majestic lettering. Ella's parents had taught her the importance of knowing her letters when she was very young. The ability to read and write was one of the things which separated the noble from the commoner. Her station may have been reduced to that of scullery maid, but Ella was anything but common.

ELLA

Of the other members of the house, only her step-sister Druzella shared Ella's love of letters. Anastasia could read well enough to fumble her way through the Lord's Book, but it was Druzella who brought literature into the house. Druzella was such a voracious reader that she never noticed when a tome or collection of poetry that she had finished went missing. Ella would read these stolen treasures by the light of the main fire, or by whatever lamplight slipped beneath the sill and into her realm.

Time spent with these books was time which brought her closer to her dead parents. Father and mother had given her the gift of letters. Her ability to read was one of the few things Ella still cherished. The rest of her treasures were on a shelf behind the main chimney. Actually, it was not a shelf, but an open area where two of the bricks had been removed. She walked around the fireplace and placed the parchment on the makeshift shelf. This side of the room was dark. Little light slipped through from the fire. Ella had so few possessions that she did not need the light. She could see them in her mind by simply running her fingers over them.

Here was the ivory brush which her mother had once brushed her hair. There was the small knife which had hung in its leather sheaf from her father's belt. There, far back in the corner where they could not fall and be damaged, were her prize possessions. A pair of shoes, slippers really, made of glass. They had been a gift from her father to her mother. The same tradesman who had fashioned their window had spun the delicate footwear.

"Footwear is the least of our worries."

As she had predicted, things had degenerated as the week had progressed. Now, with the evening of the royal ball upon them, her daughters were nearly frantic.

"But mother, these are nothing but slippers." Anastasia's voice climbed higher and higher with each whine. Her mother closed her eyes for a moment to compose herself.

"Anna, dearest, you will be wearing a full gown with no less than four underskirts. The only way anyone will see your feet is if you turn cartwheels. You could go barefoot and no one will know."

It was embarrassing, but she had used most of their meager savings on the fabric for the dresses. There was simply not enough left for the cobbler. At least not enough to afford something in time for the event.

The short preparation time was undoubtedly designed to separate those wealthy enough to be worthy of the Prince's hand from those who simply aspired to that station. Anastasia and Druzella would appear to be deserving despite their actual background. That thought had been foremost in their mother's mind since the moment the page had arrived with the announcement.

"Besides," she continued, still trying to placate her youngest daughter, "they may be slippers, but they are silken slippers."

"Silken slippers?"

"Yes, made of silk which matches your dress perfectly. Just be very careful where you step, especially while you are dancing."

Thoughts of dancing brought a smile to the young lady's face. Anastasia returned to the laces of her bustle, worries about her slippers banished from her mind.

THE SLIPPERS WERE the one thing which she did not worry about. The glass slippers would be the finest part of Ella's wardrobe. She had spent the week sneaking through the house at night, collecting what she could. She pieced together a gown from her step-sisters' rejects. She wished that some of her mother's clothing had remained in her care. Unfortunately, everything had been burned after her mother had succumbed to her illness. The only benefit was that her mother's wardrobe had been empty before the three harpies had taken up residence in the house.

She had worked on her dress each day, sleeping only a few hours before turning back to the needle and thread. The night before the ball, Ella had rushed through her chores to make sure that she had plenty of spare time. She felt guilty about skimping on the housework, but it was the first time in years that she had done so.

Every night she had cleaned, healthy or sick, no matter how tired she was.

Unlike her step-sisters, Ella's evening attire was prepared before the sun rose on the morning of the ball. She did not rush through her tasks so she would have extra time to prepare. She rushed through her tasks so she could remove her dress, her slippers, and herself from the house. She snuck out before the sunrise, her arms wrapped tightly around a bundle. She slipped through the back field to the old stable. The horses and the rest of the livestock were long gone. It had been months since Ella had visited the stables. The memories which arose were too painful. Her father in his riding gear, her mother dressed for travel, these images were more than she could handle.

This day, however, she vowed to deal with the ghosts of her past in order to prepare for her future. She placed her clothing in the empty tack room, making sure the glass slippers were safe. She then moved to one of the stalls to sleep. Despite the length of time since she had been there, the stables were close to immaculate. There were some spider-webs in the corners, a little dust on the floor. Ella's main problem was that when she had swept out the stables she had removed all of the straw. Now there was nothing for her to lie on but the rough hewn wood of the floor. Still, the floor was no less comfortable than the bricks of the hearth which she was used to.

DRUZELLA WATCHED her sister pace the floor. Anastasia had found what she determined to be a slight imperfection in one of the under-skirts of her gown. Their mother sat near the window, the area of the house with the most light, and mended the skirt with needle and thread.

The room was warm. Dust motes danced in the rays of sunlight streaming through the window. Anastasia's steady step had a soporific affect. Druzella stifled a yawn. Neither girl had been able to sleep the previous night. Their excitement had kept them awake, whispering to each other long after the lamps had been extinguished for the night. The excitement of the upcoming evening should have been enough to keep the girls awake. Perhaps they would perk up when the carriage which their mother had arranged for arrived. Until then, the lack of anything to do conspired to drive Druzella's chin down against her chest and her lids closed.

Ella woke refreshed and alert after sleeping most of the day in the old stable. The faint musk of horses still clung to the stall where she rested. The scent was somehow warm and comforting. Although part of her longed to stay where she was, Ella forced herself to move. She gained energy from her motion. Soon she was striding down to the stream, a bucket in either hand.

It would have been easier to bathe in the slow moving water which marked the far boundary of the estate. The chances of being seen by anyone were almost nonexistent. Still, modesty forced her to fill the buckets and carry them back to the trough. A lady would not stoop to bathing in the open. Her mother would never have done so.

Three trips to the stream was enough to fill the trough. Ella searched the area around the stable once more before disrobing. The water was cold enough to draw a gasp from the young woman. The breeze raised goose-flesh wherever it touched her. She bathed quickly, using a rag and a piece of harsh soap to scrub the accumulated dirt and ashes from her body, her face, and her hair.

She put on her best shift. Although mended many times and gray from age, it was better by far than what she wore while cleaning her father's house. She went to the shelf and retrieved her hairbrush. Lacking a mirror, she turned to the only reflective surface available-- the water in the trough.

Her hair was a mass of tangles. The water had loosed some of the knots, but Ella still struggled to pull the bristles through her hair. She winced and cried out as a large clump tore itself free. She was forced to switch from the long strokes that she remembered from her mother's loving touch to short tugs and yanks.

The sun had begun to slink towards the horizon before Ella finished with her hair. She tied it back with a simple blue ribbon, then hurriedly finished dressing. The dress was light blue. She had found the bolt of cloth lying in the bottom of a closet in her step-mother's sewing room. Her gown was nothing fancy, but it was impressive. Ella skills as a seamstress surpassed all the other women in the house. The gown's unadorned simplicity was limited not by the skill of the seamstress, but by the lack of materials and the fact that Ella had been working in almost total darkness.

The clatter of a horse drawn carriage made Ella turn. She ran to the shelf where she had hidden her possessions. She looked at her mother's slippers, then tucked them in with the rest of the items. Running in such footwear was sure to damage it. She hurried back up the hill to the main house.

THE CLATTER of the carriage interrupted the flurry of activity in the house. Each woman paused momentarily. The house was completely still for a few seconds.

"They are here!"

Anastasia's mother frowned the young girl back into silence. She examined her younger daughter, adjusted one hem, then turned to Druzella. Her older daughter also passed muster. She touched her own hair to ensure that all was well. Then she fixed a smile on her lips and turned to the door. The carriage would be there soon.

THE CARRIAGE WOULD BE THERE SOON. Ella could see the dust it kicked up pluming beyond the bend in the road. She hiked her skirts and ran across the lawn. She had planned everything. From the moment she read the announcement, her mind had been working furiously. Her plan had worked perfectly, but her plan ended at this point. She had not thought beyond preparing for the ball. She had no idea what would happen now.

She had no delusions that this would bring her closer to her step-family. If anything, this would infuriate her step-mother. It would not matter if her step-mother was angry or not. So long as there was someone else in the house, the old witch's hands would be tied. She would never vent her anger in front of a stranger. Even more important, there was no way that she could refuse to allow Ella to accompany them to the ball. The proclamation had specifically stated that all girls of marble age should attend.

THE CARRIAGE REIGNED to a halt before the main door. Both girls started forward. A look from their mother forced them back into their seats. Anastasia was quivering, unable to keep still. Even Druzella was having a difficult time remaining still. Their mother stood just inside the door. She smiled at her daughters, putting on a brave face while mentally recording their faults. The coachman knocked on the door.

THE REAR DOOR which led from the kitchen to the rear lands opened. Ella stepped inside. She leaned carefully against the wall and slipped her mother's shoes on, first one foot, then the other. They slid on easily.

Ella smiled. She had worried that the slippers would not fit. Instead, the were surprisingly comfortable. It was as if her mother was smiling down on her. She walked carefully from the kitchen into the main hall, walking in her mother's footsteps while wearing her mother's footwear.

THE MAIN DOOR OPENED WIDE. The coachman bowed low. He rose, his face a mask of polite submissiveness. The look remained in place for a moment, then his jaw dropped open. The woman who had opened the door was saying something to him, but the words did not register. He could only stare past the woman, past the two young ladies

ELLA

seated in the next room, and at the person who was walking up the hall towards them.

Anastasia looked questioningly at her sister. Were they supposed to get up now, or wait for someone to escort them to the door? Their mother stood next to the coachman, trying to get his attention. He looked very fine in his red livery. This did nothing to appease their mother's annoyance. Finally, she turned to follow the coachman's gaze. She abandoned all pretense of civility.

"You!" she screamed.

The girls turned to see their step-sister shambling towards them. Neither girl had glimpsed their step-father's daughter for years. They knew that she came up each evening to clean the house. They were not sure why she chose to live in the cellar instead of one of the empty rooms upstairs. The sisters had spoken of this only once. Druzella secretly thought that the exile had been forced upon Ella by their mother. Anastasia claimed that their was not proof of this. Sensing that the topic would drive their mother into a rage, the girls had never broached the subject again.

Ella was dressed in a mad mishmash of clothing. Loops of blue fabric had been sewn together to make an approximation of an evening gown. One shoulder had slipped low, exposing the pale flesh of Ella's upper arm and the swell of her bosom. Her hair stood up like a bramble bush. A blue ribbon hung from one side.

Worst of all were her feet.

Ella's feet were nearly black with soil. She looked as if she had been running in mud and then allowed the mud to dry. The filth was visible despite the shoes she wore, as the shoes were transparent. They seemed to be made of glass. They were far too small. Somehow the girl had managed to wedge her feet into them. The narrowness of the shoes made walking almost impossible. Ella shambled up the hall towards the small group. There was a horrible crack, then a crunching sound. The shoe on her left foot shattered. Ella's next step sliced her foot. Blood began to seep through tiny cuts, mixing with the dirt. Each step left a print composed of soil and blood on the floor which she herself had cleaned.

"What?" The coachman's voice failed him.

"I am ready." Ella said plainly. The words were barely louder than a whisper. The girls had to strain to hear her.

"For what?" Ella looked into her step-mother's eyes. She had not expected any resistance.

"For the ball." She tried to clear her throat. She longed to speak clearly and with conviction, but her voice was rusty from years of disuse. She stood tall, her head high, her frame erect.

The coachman coughed and turned away.

Her step-mother looked at her for a moment, then turned back to the coachman.

"My daughters and I are ready."

The statement was simple, but the emphasis on the first word spoke volumes. Ella pursed her lips, then bit her lower lip hard enough to draw blood. She would not cry before this woman. She would not allow the hot tears welling in her eyes to fall.

She had expected denial. She had expected laughter. She had not prepared herself to be dismissed so casually.

She would not accept this.

Druzella and Anastasia stood as one. Their mother's words had been their cure to move. Neither girl cared for escorts or proper etiquette. They simply wanted to leave the uncomfortable scene behind.

"No."

The word was no more audible than anything she had said previously. This time, however, the word had force behind it.

Three step brought her to where her step-sisters stood. Their gowned and perfumed backs blocked Ella's view of the matron at the door. She pushed her way between them roughly. Druzella fell back against her chair. Anastasia cried out as her ankle twisted. She fell, her head striking the end table with a hollow thunk.

"Anna?" Druzella's voice was shaky. She dropped to her knees beside her sister. A crimson puddle was forming beneath the blonde curls. She shook her sister, but got no response.

"Anna?"

It took two more steps for Ella to cross the room. The coachman shrank back against the door-frame. Her step-mother did not flinch.

"No is right," she said. Her lip curled into a sneer. "No, you will not be going to the ball. Not with your hair a tangled bird's nest, not in that horrid excuse for a dress, and not in those wretched slippers."

Ella looked down at her feet. Both bled freely. The toe of the right shoe was still intact. A think crimson puddle could be seen through the glass. The shoes were ruined.

How had this happened?

She looked up at her step-mother.

"Get back downstairs."

The words were cold, full of disgust.

"You, you did this." Ella's voice was soft, timid.

"You did this to yourself. I tried to make you into something but you could not live up to…"

The words were cut off by Druzella's scream. All eyes turned to Anastasia for a moment. Druzella had her sister's head cradled in her lap. The front of Druzella's gown was smeared with blood and something else, something which resembled a gray pudding.

As soon as her step-mother looked away, Ella was able to act. The spell which had held her in place broke. Her mother's prize possession was ruined.

But she still had her father's.

The knife had been resting in a fold of the dress. It was warm from being against her skin. Ella brought it up with one quick movement. The blade was still sharp despite years of being neglected.

Her step-mother had started to run towards her daughters when the blade flashed. Her motion carried her directly into Ella's upward thrust. The knife passed easily into the flesh beneath her chin and lodged in her throat. She old woman fell back, clawing at the handle. Her breath wheezed around the blade. She slid down the wall, fell forward, and was still.

The coachman turned and ran.

Druzella was keening, rocking her sister's lifeless form. She was unaware of what had transpired at the door. She did not notice her mother's demise.

She did not notice when Ella walked up behind her.

"Stop that."

"No, no, no. Anna, no."

Ella placed her hands around her step-sister's neck.

"Stop that noise."

"Oh, no, Anna."

"Do not pollute my father's house with your noise."

Her voice was clear now. Druzella looked up at her step-sister, then down at her lost sister. She closed her eyes.

Ella squeezed until Druzella stopped crying.

Then the house was silent.

ELLA DID NOT KNOW how long she sat there. Her once fine dress had soaked up much of Anastasia's blood. The world outside the glass window was dark. The carriage was long gone.

She wondered how she would get to the ball.

Ella stood. Druzella' body, which had been leaning against her, slumped to the floor. Ella walked to the lamp and lit it. Blood dripped from her skirts, staining the wood floor.

It would take a lot of work to clean her father's house.

She heard a noise outside. Her head snapped up. Maybe the carriage had come back.

Instead of the carriage, she saw a monster. It was dirty, covered in blood and gore. Ella yelped. She leaned forward.

It was no monster. It was her own reflection in the glass.

Was this what people saw when they looked at her? Was this why she had lived beneath the house for so many years? Was this why her step-mother had never cared for her the way she cared for her own daughters?

Was this why her father had remarried?

Was this why her mother had left?

ELLA

Ella looked around the shambles of the room. The blood from Anastasia's head had begun to grow tacky at the edges. It had probably seemed into the floor joists. Who knew what lay beneath her stepmother.

Ella sighed, resigning herself to her next task. She walked over to the staircase and sat. She chose the stairs which led up to the sleeping chambers for her chair. She leaned her back against the wall. The stairs to the cellar were out of her view.

She would have to clean this, fix it, make it right.

Ella lifted one foot and removed one of the shards of glass which still clung to it. She placed the glass against her wrist and carefully, deliberately, cleansed it all.

REMEDY

Inevitably, there was a knock on the door. Expected, anticipated, and yes dreaded, the knock was timid, a cautious rapping. If I hadn't been waiting for it, I doubt that I would have heard it at all.

Not that it really mattered. I'd known that someone was in the area for the last fifteen minutes. The trees and their residents had let me know with their silence. And it wasn't as if I received so many callers that one would go unnoticed.

I sighed heavily, then heaved myself to my feet. I shuffled past the mantle, pretending that the creaking sounds I heard were the floorboards and not my old bones protesting the movement. Above this common noise and through the heavy oak door I could hear them whisper.

"She's probably not in."

"Of course she's in, where else would she be?"

"Well, I don't see a car."

"Maybe she doesn't have one."

"Who doesn't own a car?"

"Lots of people."

"OK, in the city and the closer suburbs maybe, but out here?"

I had reached the entrance, but decided against opening it just yet.

Perhaps it would be a good idea to find out who was out there and what they wanted first. I thought I recognized one of the voices.

"I thought you wanted to take care of this. If you're just going to chicken out then we can just go."

"No...I just."

"It's up to you Kirsten, but you have to decide. I'm not going to sit out here all night."

I opened the door, just as one of the women moved to knock again. Her hand, already in motion, carried her off balance when it met no resistance. I stepped back as her knuckles past through the air inches from my face.

"Oh!"

I squinted into the darkness. Two young women stood on my stoop. Both wore flowing skirts, peasant blouses, and detailed corsets. One had a garland of flowers in her hair, while the other's head was hidden by the hood of her cloak.

Renaissance Faire garb, now I knew where they were from. The one with the flowers looked familiar. I have always been great with faces, but lousy with names. Former client, name started with an R, vaguely Biblical.

"Rebecca, nice to see you again."

Her head snapped up. She met my eyes, held my gaze. That was good.

"And you must be Kirsten."

I turned so they would not see the smile spurred by their surprise.

"Come in, come in," I said as I stumped back to the hearth. "Close the door, grab some chairs from the table, have a seat."

I dropped back into the overstuffed hair I had been sitting in before the knocking. The two paused a moment in the doorway. Rebecca shot Kirsten a look.

Decide now.

They came in.

"What brings the two of you to my home?" It took me a moment to recall why Rebecca had first visited me. I knew it involved a tincture. Had someone been sick? No, that wasn't it. She hadn't been looking to end a pregnancy, to start one? No, but close.

"And how is your young paramour?"

Rebecca blushed, then extended her hand. An impressive diamond ring squatted on her finger.

"We've been together for two years now. He proposed this Spring."

Two years? Had it really been that long?

"I assume that means that the need is not yours." I turned an expectant eye to her friend.

Even inside, it was difficult to make out Kirsten's features. She sat straight up in her seat, which placed her just outside the reach of the lamp by my chair. The hood had fallen back a bit, providing hints of high cheekbones and full lips turned down at the corners.

"Do you have a beau of your own?"

Even in the gloom, I could see her scowl. She leaned forward, hands on knees.

"I have to know, are you real?"

I took a beat before answering. I made a big show of rolling up my sleeve and pinching the skin of my arm. I cocked an eyebrow.

"No, I mean can you really do what people say you can? Can you do magic?"

"Krissy!" Rebecca hissed.

"Don't call me that."

The exchange went mostly unnoticed. I stayed in place, but her words rocked me. *People*? Were people actually talking about me? No one in the village said anything when I shopped. Everyone seemed perfectly pleasant. Were the rumors starting again? Was I going to have to give up my treasured little plot of land? Or was it just among the cosplayers at the Faire?

"Why don't you tell me what you need, and I'll see what I can do."

"There's a boy…" she trailed off. If I had a nickel for every time a tale started with *There's a boy*.

I glanced at Rebecca. She shook her head. Curious.

"There's a boy, Roger. I want him to leave me alone."

Kirsten sat back. She looked exhausted, telling me that much had sapped her strength.

"He won't leave her alone." Rebecca was a true friend, picking up the thread. "She's told him again and again that she's not interested, but he won't take no for an answer. He keeps finding ways to be alone with her—"

"I'm afraid."

THOSE WORDS CHILLED ME. I remembered a time, almost half a century and a thousand miles away. I remembered the looks, the suspicion. I remembered the fear.

Kirsten continued with her story. I tried to listen; my eyes focused on her but I was seeing a fishing captain — broad shoulders, hands rough from tying ropes and hauling nets. Rough hands that dealt out rough punishment to anyone who dared cross him. Eyes the color of a storm at sea. Cold eyes, never laughing, only searching out for the next thing he wanted to possess.

I'd been seventeen when those eyes swept me up the first time. I had seen them cloud over with anger the first time I had pulled away from those hands and every time after that I had told him no.

We were a small community, but not one so close knit that anyone would move to stand against him. I had been left to fend for myself.

Everyone was shocked when the calm seas had turned gray, the sky black, and the waves swept over the gunwales and dragged him down. The rest of his crew was fine. He was never seen again.

No one could believe that such a strong swimmer, someone who had lived on the ocean since a boy, could have met such an end. Rumors spread. The small community had done nothing to help one of their own, but they were quick to accuse, ostracize.

I left before they could decide to condemn.

Now, half a century later, I sat in a small home far away from the ocean. The wind in the trees was soothing, but I missed the sound of the waves lapping against the shore every day. I sat, listening to a young woman describe the same man. Not the *same* man, but one so similar I could paste the features of my past on to her future.

"Can you help?" she asked.

I waited a long moment. I looked from one to the other. I thought about the ingredients I had in the house, what I would need, how far I would have to go to get them.

"I can help." Both women sagged in the chairs. "It will take me a week or two to get what I need. In that time, I'll need a few things from you."

"Anything," Kirsten said, reaching for a small pouch at her waist. I waved her away.

"I'll need to know what he looks like. You'll have to point him out to me at some point."

"I can do better than that," Rebeca said. She slipped a phone from inside her bodice. "I've got pictures."

"Excellent. The other thing is that you will have to take a break from the Faire. You'll have to make sure that you are elsewhere in two weeks. Somewhere where you will be seen"

Kirsten nodded. Rebecca's eyes narrowed. If she wondered what I had planned, she didn't say anything. Finally, she agreed.

"Good." I stood, pointed to the door. "I had better get started."

"Do you…"

"No, I don't require help nor payment. Just a little solitude so I can work."

ADWENIA'S UNCONVENTIONAL OVEN

"Do not pay the ticket price for that," Margery said, her voice a shrill whisper. "Never pay the ticket price."

Adwenia hated to haggle.

To be honest, she was not a fan of the whole garage sale experience. Pieces of other people's lives strewn about suburban lawns for others to pick over. Family histories tagged with yellow dots, prices inked on them in sharpie. How could you put a price on someone's life?

More importantly, how could you look at that price, then look someone in the eye and say that it was too high?

Adwenia had allowed herself to be dragged along with Margery and the rest of the yard sale scavengers. The ladies piled into Margery's minivan and cruised up and down the side streets, eyes peeled for the handmade signs and the balloons which marked the carcasses of another suburban dweller's capitalistic dream. They would pull up as close as possible to the tent city of card tables and folding chairs then swoop down like buzzards.

Normally Adwenia would have avoided what the other ladies referred to as a "shop hop." In fact, she had tried to bow out on the day in question, but Margery had convinced her to go along with one simple question:

"What else do you have to do?"

The only answers she could come up with involved binge watching Netflix, playing with the cats, and trying to decide which delivery place to get dinner from. Going out on the yard sale quest would at least delay those things.

Which was how she ended up standing on the front lawn of some old lady's house, dickering with some old lady's grandson about the price of a toaster oven.

The toaster oven, when you stopped to think about it, was really a device from another time. Like the rotary phone, the answering machine, and the tape deck, it was a technological anachronism. The years had come and gone, new things had been invented, and these items were relegated to the 'isn't that quaint' status.

"The honest truth is that most people aren't going to need a toaster oven."

Adwenia spoke these words to the disinterested young man wearing a tee shirt for a band she had never heard of who was manning the cash box. She felt a little guilty saying it because *she* actually needed a toaster oven. She had a perfectly good stove that she rarely used. It seemed a waste to heat it up when you were cooking for one. It was far easier to warm something up in the microwave.

Then her microwave had died. She spent a week looking at ads for various appliance stores. Replacing it wouldn't be too expensive, a couple hundred dollars at the most. Still, it was a couple hundred dollars that she didn't have to blow at the moment.

The toaster oven would fit her needs perfectly.

It would allow her to save up and get a really good microwave, rather than some cheap thing that would have to be replaced in a few months.

Besides, it made toast. It had been a long time since she had owned a toaster.

"Yeah, I guess you're right," the kid said. "I guess we could take five bucks for it."

Adwenia pulled a wad of singles out of her pocket, peeled off five

ADWENIA'S UNCONVENTIONAL OVEN

crumpled bills, and handed them over. The young man placed them in the metal box at his feet.

"Thank you," she said.

"No worries. Besides, it's not like they'll let Grams have it where she's going anyway."

Adwenia just nodded and hurried back to the minivan with her prize.

It took a while for the other ladies to join her. Each had a pile of prizes. Margery had scored an entire eight piece serving set of slightly chipped dishes. The women cackled to one another about the bargains that they had made, what they were going to do with their new purchases, who had landed the biggest score. The whole thing reinforced the image of carrion birds picking over bones.

THE REST of the afternoon was pure drudgery. The minivan stopped at five more houses. One featured nothing but baby clothes. Another was filled with guys who looked like lumberjacks. There was so much flannel, retro eyewear, and facial hair that the ladies could barely get a look at the items that were for sale. Fortunately, the card tables were filled with old record albums and used action figures — nothing that the ladies were interested in.

"Stupid hipsters," said one of the ladies whose name Adwenia had forgotten. "I'll never understand people who try so hard to look like individuals by looking like everyone else."

Adwenia looked that the almost-matching jeans and sweaters that the ladies were wearing and kept her mouth shut.

The ladies finally ran out of money, interest, or both and decided to pack it in. Adwenia thanked them for the afternoon.

"We'll have to do this again sometime soon," Margery said through the driver's side window.

Adwenia suppressed a shudder.

"Yes indeed," . She hurried into her apartment, carrying her prize like a newborn.

Once inside, she tossed her purse and keys on the nearest chair and headed straight to the kitchen. She placed the toaster oven in the spot which had once held her microwave.

She paused with the plug in one hand. *How old was this thing? Would it even work? What if it started a fire?*

Adwenia shook herself. The kid had said that they were getting rid of things from his grandmother's because she would not need them, not because they were old or didn't work. Besides, how would she find out if it functioned if she didn't plug the darn thing in?

She pushed the plug into the socket.

Nothing happened.

Adwenia took this as a good sign. There were two dials on the right of the glass door. One was centered over an orange area marked like the temperature dial of an oven. Beneath it was a list of cooking times for various items. The lower half, of this area had a brown label with a color gradient which read "Light" to "Dark."

Directly in-between was the button to make toast.

Adwenia crossed her fingers and pushed the button down.

No sparks shot out of the wall. The room was not plunged into darkness by a blown fuse. The coils inside the oven, clearly visible through the spotless glass, began to glow a soft orange.

She waited while the little oven ran through its cycle. The button popped up. She shrugged and opened the door. This caused the wire tray to move forward. What a smart little gadget!

Adwenia placed a piece of bread on the tray and closed the door. She selected a medium setting for the first piece of toast and pushed the button again. While she waited, she ran her hand over the spotless chrome. If not for the little yello price sticker, the toaster oven could have been brand new.

She was startled out of her musing by the smell of something burning. She snatched open the door. A small plume of black smoke poured out. The bread had turned into soft goop that dripped down through the wire of the rack on to the heating element.

Adwenia opened the window to let the smoke out. She reached in to pull out the mess, but it was still too warm to touch. Her stomach growled. She grabbed an apple from the basket by the fridge and ate it while examining the bread. It was still well before the Best If Used By

ADWENIA'S UNCONVENTIONAL OVEN

date on the packaging. She opened the bag and sniffed it. Did she detect a slight whiff of mold?

She decided to play it safe and toss the remainder of the loaf in the trash. Then she spent the better part of a half an hour scrubbing the remnants of failed toast off of the rack and the heating element. By the time she was done she was no longer hungry.

She left the rack to dry, closed the little glass door, and went to watch some television.

A FEW DAYS passed before she was once again home for dinner. The downside to living alone was that Adwenia rarely felt the urge to cook. She was quite a good cook, but it seemed a waste to spend all that time working on something when she was just going to eat alone. It was a lot easier to pop something in the microwave.

At least it had been.

Adwenia came home, kicked off her shoes, and went straight to the kitchen. She was absolutely famished. She took two tortillas out of the fridge, added a handful of cheese, and turned to the counter. Maybe they would be good toasted. She wrapped the concoctions in tin foil and popped them into the toaster oven. She turned the knob to 350 and went to change.

She promptly forgot about the toaster oven and its contents.

She was getting herself a glass of water and wondering what to have for dinner when she remembered the cheese tacos. Adwenia rushed to the little oven and pulled open the door. Some part of her mind asked why the room wasn't filling up with smoke from the burnt food. She expected to find the contents a blackened mess. What she saw was even more puzzling.

Sitting on the tray was a pile of white powder. Resting in the powder were yellowish-white clumps. She reached in and touched one, pulling her finger back quickly. The foil was hot, the clumps radiated heat.

Adwenia slipped an oven mitt over her hand and removed the foil.

She sniffed it. It had a faint, vaguely dairy smell, like cottage cheese, but different. She tasted it.

It wasn't bad.

She popped it into her mouth.

It reminded her of the cheese curds she sometimes had at a nearby restaurant. She reached back into the toaster oven, sifting through the coarse powder. It was light, clinging to her damp fingertips in clumps.

An idea started to form in her mind. She swept the contents of the toaster oven into her hand, and deposited them in the sink. She searched her cupboard for something to test her theory.

As usual, the cupboards were empty. Still, she managed to scrounge up crackers, apple sauce, breakfast cereal, and peanut butter. Each went into the toaster oven for twenty minutes. She ended up with a dusting of flour and baking soda, a pile of apple chunks, some odd, oozing chemicals dusted in sugar, and a small fire caused by the oil dripping off of the peanuts.

The results of her experiments made it impossible for her to ignore the facts. There was something horribly wrong with the toaster oven. It did not cook food. It wouldn't even make toast.

Adwenia's five dollar find returned matter to its previous state.

She would not have accepted this insane notion that her toaster oven was some sort of matter transformation machine if not for her last experiment. She would have found some way to convince herself that there was something wrong with the processed food which she placed in the toaster oven, then found some other reason for never using it again.

Instead, perversely, she tried to cook an egg.

Adwenia had been raised in the suburbs. She had no hard knowledge of animal husbandry. However, it did not take a degree in biology or even a Google search to determine that five minutes at 350 had reduced the egg to a glob of rooster spermatozoa and a gallinaceous ovum.

She threw up into the sink for five minutes, unplugged the appliance, and crawled into bed where she stayed for three days.

"Adwenia? Are you still alive?"

Margery's voice grated like a rusty nail on glass. As much as she just wanted to be left alone, Adwenia knew the only way to get her friend to stop the racket was to answer her.

"I'm in the bedroom. I'll be out in a minute." She tore off the sweat suit she had been living in for three days. There was no time to shower, so she slipped on fresh clothing and tried to tame her hair. Beyond the bedroom door, she could hear the clank and clatter of Margery moving about the house.

"What are you doing here?" Adwenia said when she finally stumbled into the living room. Her hand went to the wall to steady herself as well as confirm that there were no other aspects of the universe that were playing fast and loose with the rules. Margery sat on the couch, staring at her.

Adwenia waited for her revert to a pile of goo or perhaps devolve into some ape creature.

"My God, are you OK?"

"Yes," Adwenia answered automatically. "I'm fine."

"Well you look like crap. No wonder you've been calling in. Is it the flu?"

She started to say no, but how would she answer the next question? *Oh, I'm OK physically, but my mind took a vacation from reality when my toaster oven started acting like a time machine.* That would go over well.

"Yeah, I must have picked up something while we were out."

There was a moment of silence, then Adwenia giggled. Margery's expression went from one of affront to concern.

"You certainly don't look well."

"Thanks." Adwenia dropped into a chair. She concentrated on stifling the bout of laughter which threatened to erupt. Hysteria and madness were just around that corner.

"Well don't worry, I've got just the thing to make you feel all better."

Adwenia got as far as "I really don't" when there was a horrible crash from the kitchen. Both women turned to look at the tiny food prep area. The sound repeated, the jangling of something banging on metal.

A horrible screeching erupted from the room. Something was shrieking in pain, over and over.

"What did you do?" Adwenia screamed at her friend.

"Nothing!" she hollered back, her voice raised over the sounds of anguish. "I'm just warming up some soup for you."

"What kind of soup?" Adwenia asked, but Margery was lost, staring wide eyed at the toaster oven. The little steel box was thrashing, jumping from one spot to another on the counter.

Adwenia, hands over her ears in a vain attempt to block out the horrible screeching sounds coming from the kitchen, rushed from the room. She pushed past Margery, who was standing dumbstruck in the doorway.

"I don't know…I just…"

The sound was coming from the far end of the counter. The toaster oven rocked and bucked, thrashing like a thing possessed.

Figures.

"I just wanted you to feel better. My mom always said that the best solution to any ailment was—"

"What *kind* of soup?"

"Chicken noodle. Homemade."

Adwenia turned away, not wanting to see the half formed chicken, boiling in its own juices, which was sure to burst out of the toaster oven at any moment. She slid back down into the chair, her head bowed. She jammed her fists against her ears to shut out the sound.

ABOUT THE AUTHOR

Michael Cieslak is a lifetime reader and writer of horror, mystery, and speculative fiction. A native of Detroit, he lives in a house covered in Halloween decorations in October and dragons the rest of the year. He is an officer in the Great Lakes Association of Horror Writers and is the editor of the Erie Tales anthologies. His works have appeared in a number of collections including *DOA: Extreme Horror*, *Dead Science*, *Vicious Verses and Reanimated Rhymes*, the GLAHW anthologies, *Alter Egos Vol 1*, *Pan's Guide for New Pioneers* (a supplement for the Pugmire RPG), and the collaborative steampunk novel *Army of Brass*. *Urbane Decay*, a collection of Michael's short fiction is now available. He reviews horror movies for the Dead On Movie Reviews podcast.

Michael is the Editor in Chief of Dragon's Roost Press (thedragonsroost.biz).

- facebook.com/michael.cieslak.9
- instagram.com/cieslak.michael
- amazon.com/stores/Michael-Cieslak/author/B00SWE25LI

DRAGON'S ROOST PRESS

DRAGON'S ROOST PRESS is the fever dream brainchild of dark speculative fiction author Michael Cieslak. Since 2014, their goal has been to find the best speculative fiction authors and share their work with the public. For more information about Dragon's Roost Press and their publications, please visit:

HTTP://WWW.THEDRAGONSROOST.BIZ

Acknowledgments

The author would like to thank the following:

David Hayes for editorial excellence and everlasting friendship.

Source Point Press for the original publication of this collection.

The Great Lakes Association of Horror Writers. Your work is inspirational, your camaraderie priceless.

My family for the continuing support.

All the canine companions who have graced me with their love.

And especially my wife Ruth for being the most important part of my life.

Made in the USA
Monee, IL
17 October 2023